I0738849

# *Valkyrie*

— ◆ —

## MIKE SIMS

**Volume two of the Vickie series**

Published by Mazzaroth
Katy, TX

www.Mazzaroth.net

Published in the United States of America

ISBN: 978-0-9982983-8-2
Fiction / General

To Laura and Gary Neal, Keith and Cheryl Partney, as well
as Kim and Gerald Svetlik.

# ACKNOWLEDGMENTS

Thank you, Nicole Andani, for your wisdom and support in making this book and its series a reality.

C O N T E N T S

# Progress

<hr>

Vickie sits in her office staring out the window thinking, *My life has been a recipe for disaster, but yet I hunger for it.* She sits at her desk and picks up the Lazarus Game paper, staring at the Valkyrie symbol on it. She thinks, *Why would people play games with other people? Seems my whole life people have tried to play games with me. It seems that games are the nature of people. Maybe not the nature but boredom that rules their sense of being decent. Look at how much we sell because of boredom. An entire industry of marketing exists to keep people occupied. Like boredom was some kind of mental disease to be fought. Our industry spends more on advertising and marketing than we do fighting cancer. It is the way of the world, so be it.* She drops the game paper and begins to thumb through statistics on the computer. After a while Vickie rubs her eyes and stands to look out the window some more.

John Taylor, the marketing director, walks in. "Has anything moved out there."

Vickie turns around and smiles. "I am keeping an eye on it."

"Here are the results of the Spinner campaign."

"Great, more things to read."

John frowns with a half smile. "My mom asked about you the other day."

"She feeling like berating someone?"

John laughs. "No, she wanted to know how you were."

"And how am I?"

"You are doing just fine."

"I am glad to hear that about me."

"Can I ask you question?"

"You just did, sure."

"You don't date much, do you?"

"Why, John, delving into my love life?"

John's face turns red as he begins to stutter. Vickie replies, "There was another John in college. My God, I make it sound like I am a prostitute. Anyway, that was the only one." Vickie looks down at her desk. "He destroyed himself." John has a concerned look on his face. "I am sorry I brought it up." Vickie looks up. "No, it is all right. He was an alcoholic." John looks down. "Wow." He then notices the Lazarus Game paper and picks it up. "You are playing this too."

"No, Dan brought that."

"Yeah, he is a legend at this game. I heard about him at King's Way."

"You play it?"

"No, too rich for my blood. I don't have time for it either. Honestly, it seems cruel."

"Yeah, but these people get to experience a part of life they most likely never would." "Yeah, I get it, just not for me." John leaves as Vickie begins to look over the latest campaign results.

That evening Vickie is at her martial art school, and after her lessons she sits in front of her sensei Sato. "Sensei, have you ever heard of a game called the Lazarus Game?"

"No, what kind of game is it?"

"It is a game executives play by taking very poor people and trying to make successful people out of them. The first one to achieve it wins." Sato stares without comment. "It may seem cruel, but it allows these people to see a part of life they never would." Sato continues to be motionless as Vickie stares around and says, "It might even change their life for good." Vickie sits and quietly waits for Sato to reply, and eventually he says, "Are you trying to convince me of the game's merit or yourself?"

"I am not sure."

"How can this make anyone successful if they were not gifted to be what this game wants them to be? Success is not a matter of money or position but whether you achieved what you want to do. Making another achieve another's definition of success for the amusement of that group is a form of slavery."

"You don't think these people would benefit from having their horizons expanded?"

"You can see all horizons but must live in one."

"I understand, but how is it slavery? These people choose to play the game and take a chance on being so called successful."

"It is not the poor that are the slaves but the executives. They are the ones being played."

Vickie looks confused. "I do not understand."

"Things are never simple in the designs of men, but in nature the complexity is hidden in its simplicity." Sato stands as Vickie follows, and they bow. He leaves Vickie to ponder about what he said.

---

The next morning Dan walks in with Trevor Ortiz, who is his candidate for the Lazarus Game. Dan introduces them. "Trevor, this is Vickie, and vice versa."

Vickie shakes Trevor's hand. "Nice to meet you, Trevor."

"Nice to meet you, ma'am," replies Trevor.

"Please, Vickie."

Trevor smiles as Dan says, "Sure you don't want to partner up with me?"

Vickie says, "You afraid I might join the game to compete."

"Has crossed my mind," Dan said.

"I heard you do just fine by your lonesome," said Vickie.

"Okay, let me know if you change your mind." Dan escorts Trevor, out telling him, "You are going to have an office someday like this."

"Wow, never been in an office," says Trevor.

Vickie stares with a concerning look on her face but then gets back to work.

She brings some reports to her boss, Tom Patterson. "Here you go, Tom."

"Thank you, Vickie." She stands looking at Tom as he asks, "What is wrong?" Vickie sits down in front of Tom's desk and asks, "Do you think it is necessary for Dan to be playing this silly game here at the office?"

"Personally, I never understood it, but I guess it gives people a taste of something new and part of the pool goes to charity."

"Yeah, but the charity part is just to seem like it is for a good cause. I am not so sure this is a good thing."

"It is a waste of company time, but the advantage of it is that a lot of executives play it, and it helps a company build relationships. Used to be golf was the social business outlet, now this. What bothers you about it?"

"Like you said, it just seems like a complete waste of time."

"Now if you have problem with it, I will tell Dan not play it on company time."

Vickie looks around. "No, no, that is not necessary. I know the relations to other possible clients is important. Never mind, sorry I brought it up."

"Not to worry, always let me know your concerns." Vickie grins and leaves.

The following week Trevor delivers some reports from Dan to Vickie.

"Reports from Mr. Childers, ma'am—I mean, Vickie."

"That's better. Dan has you doing intern work?"

"He says I need to learn the work flow around here."

"Uh-huh. Is he going to have you shine his shoes next?" Trevor looks at her with a confused look. "Never mind, good luck on your venture." Trevor leaves to do more of Dan's tasks. Vickie is going on a two-week vacation—her first since she has worked there. She just needs to tidy up things while she embarks on cruise.

# C RUISE  C ONTROL

Vickie makes her way onto the cruise ship to start her vacation. She has flown to Florida to leave for a weeklong trip to various touristy stops in Mexico and then back to Florida to spend the rest of her time at a beach house. At least that is the plan. She arrives on deck awaiting departure and grabs a deck chair before they are all taken. A waiter asks if she would like a beer, and she replies, "No thank you, but I will take a virgin pina colada." She watches the land move and thinks about how far she has come in life to now be able to be here, grateful and at the same time concerned about if it will last and what else can life throw before her. But for the moment, the drink and the sun are bleaching the issues away. Vickie gets dressed up for a nice dinner, which is shared with few other people at her table. One at her table mentions he is a CFO of a large company and that his name is Zach as they introduce each other.

"Zach, can I ask you a personal question?"

"Sure, Vickie."

"Have you heard of a game called the Lazarus Game?"

Zach slows down on his eating and looks up at Vickie. "Yes, of course I have."

"Your thoughts on it?"

"I played it one year about five years ago. It seemed fun, but it really does not help people. It is just for the amusement of bullies that like to taunt and flaunt what they have in front of those who have less. If you are thinking of playing it, don't."

"I did not realize that there were people that set against it."

"Well, if I catch anyone playing it in my company, they are gone."

"Really?"

"Really."

"Obviously you are passionate about it."

"The worse hell is not just going to hell, it is experiencing heaven and then being taken to hell. It is enough for some to not want to live anymore." Zach stares at his food as if to play with it. Vickie continues with her dinner saying, "It is good."

"Nothing beats these dinners."

The dinner is pleasant and quiet till she is done. Vickie says, "Well, guys, it was nice meeting you, and I hope have a good cruise." Zach says, "Same to you."

Vickie changes to more comfortable clothing and sits out on deck to watch the stars. She thinks to herself, *There are so many of them. Wonder if there are other planets with people looking at our stars? Mom, I miss you. I hope that I am doing okay in your opinion. I wonder if my daughter looks up and sees these stars. She would be eight by now. Seems like a long time ago and another life. How did I make it through that time?* Vickie stares at the stars and drifts off from time to time. She thinks it is time to head back to her stateroom. The next day she enjoys some burgers a cruise employee is grilling. "These are very good."

"Later we will have barbecue," the employee replies.

"Not made from goat, is it?"

The employee chuckles. "No, pork ribs."

"Good." Vickie walks around the pool, and toy lands at her feet. She picks it up as a little girl runs up to her.

"Here you go, sweetie."

The little girl responds, "Thank you, lady." Her parents walk up, and her mom says, "That is very good, Veronica." Vickie smiles at the parents and asks Veronica, "So how old are you?" Veronica holds up eight fingers and says, "Eight." Vickie stares for a bit and says, "You know, I have a little girl your age."

"Where is she?" Veronica asks.

Vickie slowly and quietly says, "I don't know."

Veronica smiles. "You should find her then."

"Yes, I should."

"I'm going to be an as…as…astronnomer someday."

Vickie lights up. "Astronomer. You know, that is what I wanted to be when I was your age."

"You are not one?"

"No, I went another way in life, but I loved astronomy. I am sure you will be one and be a very good one."

Veronica's parents tell her, "Come on now, let's leave the nice lady alone." The mom looks at Vickie. "Sorry, she is so enthusatic." Vickie says, "That is okay, she reminds me of me at that age." Veronica's dad says, "It was nice to meet you." He picks up Veronica and kisses her on the cheek. "All right, you, let's play in the pool." Vickie watches them leave and start playing in the pool. Veronica sees Vickie looking at her and waves. Vickie waves back and sits down to watch a nice family having fun. She reminices about her childhood and wishes it would have been like theirs. She thinks to herself, *I am not going to sabotage my present by regretting my past. My past will not dictate how I feel about myself now. I will only let it be my tool to learn from.* Vickie starts to leave, and Veronica asks her parents something as they nod yes. Veronica runs over to Vickie and hands her the little plastic starfish toy she had. "I want you to have this. It is a starfish. Nothing to do with stars, but it is named after them."

Vickie says, "Really, I did not know that. Thank you, Veronica. I will treasure this." Veronica has a big smile on her face and runs back to her parents. Vickie walks back to her room carrying her starfish. She goes to her stateroom and sits on her bed looking at the starfish. She turns it over, and it has a red V on the back. She stares at it for a bit and puts it in her luggage.

Vickie enjoys an uneventful cruise and excursions to the ports. She manages to buy jewelry and some souveniers for the ones at work. At the end of the cruise she gathers her luggage out of customs. She notices Veronica and her family gathering theirs. Vickie reaches in her purse and pulls out the starfish. Veronica smiles and waves as Vickie waves good-bye. She arrives at her beach house and just lays on the bed looking at her starfish. She spends the week reading her new books and relaxing.

# Office Supplies

Returning to work Vickie sits at her desk holding her toy starfish from Veronica. She smiles and sits it on top of the Lazarus Game paper. Tom Patterson walks in. "Well, how was vacation?"

"It was good, I like the sea. I like looking at those stars at night. No light pollution if you go to certain parts of the ship."

"Well it is nice to have you back with us." Tom sees the starfish. "A memento of the trip?"

"A little girl gave it to me on the ship. She was so cute, I wanted to spend the whole day with her."

"Well it sounds like you had a great time. We have a new client called Mazzaroth I wanted to discuss."

"Okay, I will be right over." Tom points his finger and smiles as he leaves. Trevor walks in to hand some papers to Vickie from Dan. Trevor is very quiet and disassociative.

"What is the matter, Trevor, you missed me?" asks Vickie. Trevor stands quiet turning back and forth between leaving and standing in front of Vickie. "Trevor, what is wrong? You can talk to me, I am here if you need me." Trevor mumbles at first and then says; "I am okay, ma'am."

"Look, I have to meet with the boss, but let's talk when I am back." Trevor nods and leaves as Vickie grabs her notepad and pen to meet with Tom. She enters Tom's office, and he is already meeting with Dan at his office small conference table. Vickie sits down, and Dan says, "Hey, Vic, how was vacation?"

"It was good, I was away from you for a while," replies Vickie.

"Not nice," says Dan.

Tom says, "C'mon, guys, lets get to it. Vickie, to catch you up, we have a production company called Mazzaroth that uses a web domain of Mazzaroth.net. They specialize in books, TV shows. What they need for us is promote season four of their successful tv show *Destiny*. Now this is a reverse of what we usually do as you know. We usually sell advertising to TV shows for clients, but our recent work on campaigns has led them try the opposite."

"Basically they want to buy our advertisers by letting us manage things," concludes Vickie.

"Exact-a–mundo," says Dan. "I have analyzed their show, and it is like a variety show where different characters experience a new situation each episode. There is no continuity to the show, each is different."

"That presents a problem as we are not sure how each episode will be received."

"Right metrics are out the window on this one."

Tom says, "Vickie, here is the copy of the Mazz file. Give it a study, and work with Dan to figure out a plan, okay, guys?"

"You got it, Tommy boy," says Dan.

"Okay," Vickie replies. Dan leaves the office. As Vickie is about to leave, she turns and asks Tom, "What is a Mazzaroth anyway?"

"The client Melinda says it is an ancient word that basically has to do with the twelve signs of the zodiac."

"Hmmm, okay."

Vickie returns to her office, and as soon as she does Trevor walks in.

"You need any office supplies, ma'am?" Vickie leans her head to one side and stares at Trevor as he says, "Sorry, Vickie."

"That's better. I don't think I need anything at the moment." Trevor stands there as Vickie says, "I guess I could use some notepads and a few pens."

"Yes, m—Vickie." He leaves as Vickie starts to read the Mazzorth file. Very quickly Trevor returns with the supplies. "Thank you, Trevor. Can you put those on my shelf for me and tell me what is on your mind?" Trevor puts them away and says, "Vickie, I not happy here."

"Not happy here or not happy with Dan?"

"With Mr. Childers." Vickie sees Dan looking at her office. "Trevor, go ahead and get back to Dan. Let's talk after work, okay?" Trevor nods his head and leaves. Vickie watches as Dan is obviously saying something to Trevor that is upsetting him. Trevor's head is slumped down and nodding. As soon as Dan finishes with Trevor, Dan walks into Vickie's office and says, "Is Trevor bothering you?"

"Not at all, he got me some office supplies."

"All right, I was just hoping he does not bother you. He has a tendency to get a puppy-dog depressive atitude once in a while. He likes to gain sympathy from people."

"Well what do you think? He is in an environment he io not familiar with and doing things he has never done before. He wants to please everyone and do a good job. Does not help when you don't lend a sympathetic ear or berate him constantly."

"Look, you may not be used to working with interns, but I have, and they are usually young and need to learn how to work in a professional environment."

"That is crap, Dan. You are just mean by nature, and the only thing you are interested in is winning that stupid game of yours."

"Whatever, Vic, I will just do things my way."

"Well you just do what you do best." Dan leaves as he directs Trevor to do more busy work.

⸺⸺▰●◄⸺⸺

That evening as the business day closes Trevor walks to his bus stop as Vickie drives next to him and says, "Get in,

Trevor, I will take you home." Trevor gets in her car and says, "Thank you, Vickie."

"Where am I going?"

"I live in Hilltown."

"I know where that area is." Vickie makes her way to that area of town as she says, "Well, Trevor, spill the beans. What is wrong with Dan?"

Trevor looks down as he says, "I don't think I can do this job anymore."

"I know Dan can be kind of tough, but you are going to find the world is full of assholes like him."

"Yeah, I know." There is a few moments of silence as Vickie asks, "There is more to it, is there?" Trevor nods. "Tell me what it is. You can trust me."

"I don't mind the work at your company, and I don't care about Mr. Childers getting onto me about things. It is the things after work that bother me."

"What things after work?"

"Sometimes after work he takes me to his house to do house work. You know, mowing the lawn, fixing up things. One entire weekend my parents and I painted his house."

"What?"

"He says it builds character and work ethic. He told me that is the reason he is successful and people like me are not. He said we are lazy and inefficient."

"That is not true. I doubt Dan has worked a real job a day of his life. From what I know of him, his family is well-to-do. He is just using you for free labor."

"I did not mind at first because I hope this takes me to a good job later."

"It won't. I am sorry to tell you this, but you are just part of their game, and when it is over, you will be left high and dry. It will be up to you to keep whatever level of success you achieved in the game. The problem is no one is going to keep you at the relationship level they can with someone like Dan."

"But I still might have a chance."

"Of course you have a chance, every lotto ticket buyer has a chance. The odds are against you though. If you want a real chance, go to college. Get an education and get a real job."

"This is my turn off to my neighborhood." Vickie follows his directions to his house in a very poor neighborhood. As they pull into his driveway, Vickie says, "Trevor, I will help you get started on an education. There are lots of things to help out there." Trevor opens the door and says, "I will think about it." He leaves, and his parents step out on the porch to greet him. Vickie thinks to herself, *He is so young.*

# S T A R G A Z E R S

B ack at work Trevor brings a box of pens and places it on Vickie's shelf.

"I did not ask for pens."

"I thought about your offer. College is just too expensive for me. I need this opportunity, but I thank you for the offer."

"It is your life, Trevor, but I think you are making a horrible mistake. My family was poor too, but I did it, and so could you." Trevor acknowledges her and leaves to other tasks. Weeks pass by as Trevor is noticeably distant and busy with Dan. Vickie's attention is purely focused on the Mazzaroth project. A meeting is held with Melinda Sandberg, the owner of Mazzaroth, and a couple of her executives Cheryl and Laura. Dan starts the meeting off. "Ms. Sandberg, ladies, I think we have a bulletproof plan to maximize revenue potential with your next season's show. We have three major sponsors who are already committed to the top ad spots. We have approached ten other companies that we feel that would compliment the ad campaigns, and they are committed. Our main advertisers have approved of the other companies to play alongside theirs, so on our end, we are set. It is just a matter of your approval to this campaign. What we plan to do is play each ad segment with a primary advertiser on segment end that ends with an emotional moment. On segments that are cliff-hangers we will have the primary ad played just before the next segment begins. This gives our primary advertiser the maximum effect for their ads. Vickie will go into the ads themselves in more detail. But using the Carson method of advertising in this case should target the age specific groups of people your show is centered around. This is a very soft flow through of advertising so not to lose any audience. If you look at the projected ad figures, this is what we think you can expect revenue-wise."

As they go over figures, the Mazzaroth client confers with her executives. Melinda says, "This is exactly what we were hoping for, and these are the advertisers we wanted. You have done a satisfactory job in this respect. What will the ads look like?" Vickie stands up and says, "We have alternate ads from some of our advertisers that were not used because of market changes. These would be reshot and polished up, but this is what we are thinking of." Vickie plays the ads on the wall TV. "The general feel is different for these ads, but it should work for your type of show. Your show is unique and carries a different story with new characters every episode, so the ads will change with them. If you look at the ad reports, it will give you the demographics and expected impact." They examine the studies as Melinda says, "I am comfortable with this campaign, and think you have a good handle on it. This is an experiment in TV show history, but we're willing to gamble a season to see how this method works. Let's move forward on this and make it happen." The deal is signed, and Trevor brings in celebratory drinks for everyone. Vickie looks up as Trevor stands there quiet. Dan says, "Thank you, Trevor, we are good now." Trevor leaves as Vickie turns her attention back to the meeting and smiles. Vickie asks, "I have a question for you, Ms. Sandberg."

"Please, Melinda."

"Yes, of course, Melinda. Mazzaroth has to do with the twelve zodiac signs correct? I ask because I used to have an interest in astronomy and stars."

"Yes it is an ancient word that deals with what is now know as the zodiac. Astrology and religions were fashioned after these signs. But they were known long before these mythologies got a hold of them. Their names and even the names of the stars are older than any known history. Almost every culture knows these constellations and their star names. Under each of the Mazzaroth twelve constellations are three subconstellations. When put together they tell a story." Everyone in the conference room is a little taken back by the explanation.

"So what is the story?"

Melinda smiles. "The story is everything." Melinda and Vickie stare at each other as Dan breaks the silence. "Well, I know I just have been educated. I am going to have to look into that more."

"Wont do you any good," Melinda says. "It is like looking at a different language. You know it is a language but not what it says. Even if you knew the language, you most likely not know the meaning because you have no context to understand it."

"I guess I will have to leave it up to the scholars to figure it out."

"I'm sure they can help you. There are only numerous interpretations, so good luck."

Vickie says, "maybe the interpretation into our terms is the failure but examining it from another mindset is required." Melinda turns to Vickie and smiles. "Exactly."

Tom says, "Well this is fascinating stuff. Let us get moving on this project." Everyone adjourns and shakes hands with each other as they leave. Melinda stops in front of Vickie to say, "If you like this type of thing, I have some books I can recommend."

"Thank you, will get with you on that."

"Very good, I think it can help like it helped me. It is important to understand where the origins of what we believe and where they came from." Melinda leaves with her executives as Tom leads them out. Dan says to Vickie, "Geez, what a case, right?"

Vickie replies, "You know, Dan, your arrogance just completely fills your ignorance, doesn't it?" Dan has a frown on his face as he walks away.

The next day Vickie recieves an e-mail from Melinda with files of information on the meaning of Mazzaroth. The e-mail reads: "Vickie, thank you for taking care of my business' ad campaign. As promised, here is information on Mazzaroth and other things. I know it sounds like a pile of hokey stuff, but trust me, it is important. At least for the reason that many believe in it. Hope this helps." Vickie replies with a thank you and prints the information to put in her bag.

⎯⎯⎯⎯⎯●⎯⎯⎯⎯⎯

That night she begins to read it, and Vickie becomes enthralled with it. She makes a trip to someone that could help here in understanding it, Professor Chan. She approaches his telescope as he is writing something down. He sees her and says, "Vickie the Valkyrie!" Vickie smiles and replies, "Hello, professor, what are you professing tonight?"

"I am working a study course on the possiblity of exoplanets."

"What is an exoplanet?"

"It is a planet that is not in our solar system."

"Would that not be likely since there are planets in this solar system?"

"Yes, but discovering them is the fun. Some might even be like earth."

"So if they were like earth, life in some form could live on them."

"Life does not have to be on earthlike conditions. Only the life adapted for earth can only live here. Other planets that are superhot or supercold could have life that can live there."

"So they would not survive if they came here?"

"Possibly, or maybe they have a much higher tolerance than us. So what brings you here?"

Vickie hands the printed material from Melinda on Mazzaroth to Professor Chan and asks, "What do you think of this?" Chan reads intently as Vickie looks at his telescope up and down. After a while Chan hands the papers to Vickie as she asks, "So what is the verdict?"

"That is interesting stuff. Many people believe in zodiacs, but what she is talking about what the zodiac was based on. It is very ancient stuff."

"What does she mean that many people believe in it?"

"Every religion and even science is based on it."

"You mean religions use the stars in their beliefs?"

"No, Ms. Newsome, they came from it, all of them. Even science is based on these things."

"Well we might have started out believing in some star myths, but we now understand them much better."

"Do we? This might prove the opposite. Maybe we understood them correctly in the beginning but then lost that understanding and made the myths."

"So what you are saying is that we fell down the mountain and are slowly climbing up?" "In some cases. Perhaps science is climbing a little faster, but it tends to think it has reached near the peak too often. Then something shakes it up, and it realizes it is nowhere near it."

"I don't understand what ancient primitive people could know that us with all our understanding cannot."

"Because you are thinking like a climber."

"How else can I think?"

"You can't, not right now."

"My brain can only think what it has been taught."

"Really? Then who taught your brain to operate your lungs and your heart? Fact is, your brain already knows how to think. All you did was learn how to operate in society and culture. You were trained like people before you were trained. It is a method of order that makes it easy for people to live by. Other cultures learn and think in other ways. We may think they are behind or savage, but they understand things we in this culture do not."

"I think I know what you are talking about. You are talking about instinct."

"Partially. I believe locked away in each on of us is the knowledge of a great many things. I believe we posses the capability to understand things on levels never dreamed of. The limit is ourselves. Some people, like the person that wrote these notes to you, is aware of it. They may not understand it completely, but they know something is there. They at least know that everything we believe is based on this lost knowledge." Vickie ponders for a bit and says, "It is not that we are looking in the wrong places but only looking."

"Now you are getting it."

"As usual, professor, it has been an education."

"Some day, Vickie, it will be reversed."

Vickie laughs. "I doubt it. You are a very smart man, professor."

"Vickie, I am just the slingshot, you are the object that will go far."

Vickie smiles. "Good night, Professor Chan."

"Good night, Vickie."

# REUNION

Vickie is at work and gets a call from her old college roommate Cindy, and they agree to meet for lunch at the park. Vickie is sitting at the park bench when Cindy arrives and says, "Hey, girlfriend! It is so good to see you." Vickie hugs Cindy and says, "God, it is so nice to see you. How have you been?"

"I am good, working as a child and young adult psychologist, and you?"

"VP of marketing for an ad company."

"Whew, VP, nice."

"So you went the child psychology route."

"Your experiences inspired me to help kids. But I get a lot of young twenty-year-olds and teenagers too."

"That is noble, and I am honored you pursued something because of me. That is very positive. How is working out for you?"

"It is very hard at times because some clients have gone through such trauma. Sometimes we can reach them, and other times it takes medication. Once in a while one gets helped, and it makes it rewarding as can be. But they are all worthwhile, even the ones that we haven't reached yet."

"There is a lot of hope in the way you talk about it."

"There should be. If you don't eternally hope, why should they?"

"So how are things with what's-her-name?"

"Lisa, good. We are still together. She is very nice, and we work together actually. She works in more crises prevention. She gets them first, and then I work with them when they are bit more stable. I took some time off after school, and this was my first job out of it."

"You are lucky, I bounced around a bit before finding this great job."

"I took my time a bit, but Lisa landed this job after a few bad ones. She brought me in, and it has been good ever since."

"My first jobs were insane, but I managed to get the goat on my last one. My current job was fairly failing until we managed to get a major account, and that led to many others."

"Sounds like you turned it around, which is why you are a VP at such a young age." "Yes, that maybe but the boss is very good too. He just needed a little more help to pull it together." They sit quiet for a while and Vickie asks, "Cindy, have you ever heard of a game called the Lazarus Game?"

"Yes, we had a kid whose dad was in it. The kid was traumatized because his dad killed himself."

"Because of the game?"

"There were many issues in that family, but the game sent his dad over the edge. His dad did very well, and they for the first time were doing financially well. However, the game ended, and the dad was not able to continue in the lifestyle he was trying to be in. They incurred a lot of debt and tax trouble—they lost everything. The dad killed himself in the garage of their house by hanging himself. His son found him and was sent to us for help. We did manage to help him but found out through his mom about this game. Vickie, if you are playing it, I would be very disappointed. Nothing that gives people false hope for entertainment purposes, and then drops them like a melon on the ground, can be good."

"No, my coworker plays it and has an intern working with us that is his zombie, as they call it. Trevor, the intern, is a young man and seems very depressed all the time. I have tried to help him, but he seems to think this is the best thing for him."

"Sad, he has no idea. You want me to talk to him?"

"If he needs it, I will take you up on it."

"Sure thing. Look, I need to get back, but it was awesome seeing you again." Vickie and Cindy hug as Vickie says, "I miss you, Cin. You take care of yourself, and let's do something sometime when we have more time." Cindy laughs. "It's a date." Vickie starts to leave and says, "Oh, tell Lisa I said hi." Cindy replies, "Sure will."

# MANAGEMENT

Vickie walks into Dan's office and closes the door. "Dan, you have a minute or two?"

"Sure, Vic, what is up?"

Vickie sits down and stares at the desk for a bit and then looks up at Dan. "It is about this game you play. I just talked with a friend of mine that is a psychologist, and she has been treating a young man who is traumatized by his dad's death due to this game. I had my reservations about this game, and now I am thinking more and more that it needs to stop. As one of the top competitors in it, I am urging you to end this cruel game."

Dan plays with his pen, looking at it, and then stares into the distance tapping his chin. Vickie intently stares at him trying to convey concern to him. Finally he looks at Vickie and says no.

"Does it mean that much to you?" asks Vickie incredulously.

"Look I am sorry about the guy that died, but most of these people live on the edge anyway. You can't be responsible for what they do to themselves. This game entertains us as executives, I won't lie. But it also gives a taste of the good life to those who would never have a chance at it. What would you give to know such a thing once in your life?"

"I don't think it gives them anything special to taste this kind of life and then be yanked from it. Happiness is not based on position or wealth in life but satisfaction with one's self. What you provide is an illusion. They see the benefits or what they think is the benefits of this lifestyle but never know that often people in your position deal with extraordinary stress at times. They think it is heaven because you sell it to them as that. When they get there, they see the money and excess but not the hardship. Then they get back to their real life and the daily struggles of making ends meet only to become lost in what it is all about."

"Oh, and what is it all about?"

"Contentment."

"I don't agree with you, Vickie. I think we are providing a valuable service to these people. Some have even been able to maintain and continue to be successful."

"I don't doubt it, but is rare. I think this game is harmful and needs to be ended."

"So what are you planning to do?"

Vickie stands up. "I am going to stop this Lazarus Game."

"That would be a big mistake."

Vickie puts her hands on her hips. "Oh, and why?"

"You know how many people play this game? You screw this up for them, you will never work in this industry again."

"Are you threatening me?"

"Maybe, if you interfere. Look, Vickie, don't take this game personally. It is just a game."

"It is not just a game, it is slavery."

Dan laughs. "They are not slaves."

"No, you are the slaves and just do not know it."

Dan chuckles more and then has a serious look. "We all have to serve someone, but I am warning you that you have no idea what you are into if you try to stop this game."

Vickie puts her hands on his desk and leans over to him. "You have no idea what you are into if you get in my way." Dan's eyes look dilated as he stares at Vickie. Vickie has a look of a statue—unmoving and unshakable. She stands up straight and walks off. Dan exhales and whispers to himself, "Wow."

Vickie walks into her boss' office and says, "Tom, we have a problem."

"Come on in and close the door."

Vickie closes the door and sits down. "I want to stop this Lazarus Game."

"Well it should not be a problem to just to make a policy that it is not allowed here in the company. I am not a fan of it, but as you know, Dan is very involved with it, and you know the relationships he brings to this company through that game."

"I know, but I am not just talking about halting it from being played here but everywhere."

"How do you even think that you could manage that? You can't manage what other companies do."

"I have to think about it. I just know this is making fools out of everyone involved, and, worse, it's really hurting people."

Tom stands and looks out his window for a while as the silence is deafening in the room. "You know what, you come up with a plan, and I will see what I can do to support it. But you do you know this means we will lose Dan?"

"He is a goofball, and we can build relationships just as good as him."

"Yeah, but, ironically, it is the game that made those for him."

Vickie stands up. "That is not a good foundation for business relationships. It only means his value is very temporal. Those relationships could evaporate just as easily as this stupid game can. I will build solid relationships based on what we do and can do here."

Tom smiles and replies, "Well you go get them, Vickie. I have every faith in you." Vickie grins as she is starting to leave. "Oh do promise me one thing though," says Tom. Vickie turns around. "What is that, Tom?"

"Don't cause too much damage, okay?"

"Can't promise that, Tom, but I will try to take that in consideration." Vickie leaves Tom's office as Tom sits down and mumbles to himself, "God help those game players."

A few weeks later Tom calls a staff meeting for upper management. Dan, Vickie, and John enter the conference room and sit down. Dan opens up with, "What is up, Tomboy?" Tom looks at the projector screen as he turns on a presentation, not acknowledging Dan. "Vickie has put together an ambitious program the past weeks. We are going to support her initiative, which is being called Bury Lazarus," Tom says. Dan's face begins to turn red as he looks at the table in anticipation of what this meeting is about. Tom continues as he moves to the first slide on the presentation, "The Lazarus Game will no longer be played at this company as part of phase one. Then we will communicate with people we know in other companies to get a feel of them ending it there also. Once we get enough companies to fall in line with this agenda, we will send out press releases denouncing the game as part of phase two. Now this game has been investigated several times before but was stonewalled by the media because no one could give them good grounds to make a story. We will give them this ground, and here is how."

Tom continues talking as Vickie looks over at Dan, who is not even looking at the presentation but intensely staring at his notepad and moving his pen end over end. Dan seems to be glossing over the meeting as Tom explains phase three. Vickie has a smug look on her face as she turns her head to the presentation but keeps Dan in her peripheral vision. Tom continues, "Phase four will then introduce legislation that this game and ones like it will be considered human trafficking punishable by law. Any questions?"

John asks, "What kind of impact are we looking at here business-wise?"

"Well I don't know. I do know it will have impact, but sometimes we need to make a stand even though it costs. As a company that is involved in being an influence over people's lives through ads, we have a responsibility to be a force for positive change just as much as a news organization does," says Tom.

"I am all for it, but you know this is going to meet with heavy opposition,"

"I realize that, but how are we going to sleep at night convincing people to buy things they don't need unless we do something that helps them sometimes?"

"Vickie, you came up with this?"

"Don't blame Vickie, she came to me for approval on this."

"It is okay, Tom," says Vickie. "Yes, John, I spoke with people that this game has damaged, and I have seen it firsthand as others have but ignored it." Dan is motionless at the indictment from Vickie. "There are people in the psychological field that horrified at this seemingly innocent game."

John turns a bit. "Wow." The room is quiet for a bit as they all know that Dan is visibly quiet, which is out of character for him. "Dan, any thoughts on this?" asks Tom. Dan sits quietly, still staring at his pad, then finally says, "Tell me this is a joke."

"No joke, Dan, we are dead serious." Dan looks up. "You people are insane. You realize how big this game is? I am one of the top people to play this game, and you are asking me to start a campaign to end it?"

"I was hoping to convince you of the merit of our cause. You would be a great person to speak against it. I know you are not convinced it is bad, but Vickie has some statistics and stories of real people it has affected."

"Spare me the stats, I work in this profession. All statistics are only good for is pitching things. You are trying to pitch a pitchman. You are being taken in by this young woman over here that probably for some womanly reason feels she needs to yank your chain for her own purposes. Don't you see it? She likes causing trouble just to solve it."

"It is nothing like that, Dan. I know in my heart this game is very wrong," says Vickie.

"Spare me, I know what motivates you. Just because you are a rape victim does not give you special privilege to tell the rest of us how to live." Tom cuts in, "Dan, that is enough!"

"How did you find out about that?" asks Vickie.

"I know people, and they can find out just about anything."

"Fine, I was raped, but that was when I was a teenager. That has nothing to do with this." "It has everything to do with this. Look, I am sorry that happened to you, but I did not rape you, and this game is not raping others. It is just a game. Your emotions are compromising your judgment."

"Well if it is just a game, then why not just stop it for the sake of harmony in this company?"

Dan stands up. "I'll give you harmony, I quit. How about that, Tom? You going to let this victim over here carry her life burdens on you? When I walk out that door, a lot of clientele leaves with me." Tom looks down for a bit and then looks up at Dan. "Dan, I already knew this would be your response. I accept your resignation." Dan looks at John and Vickie staring at him. "Okay, fine." Dan looks at Vickie. "I will fight you on this game with everything I got." Vickie leans back and smiles. "C'mon, Dan, you can do better than that. I raise your got with one have, and you can ride this game to the pit." Dan's face turns red with anger as he storms out of the room. John looks down at the table. "Wow." Tom says, "Vickie, I guess phase one has begun."

"Yes, it has." Vickie stares through the glass watching Dan throw his personal stuff into a box in his office.

# Let the Games Begin

A few days later Tom calls Vickie and John in his office. "Dan has hired into one of our competitors, and three of our clients have already moved to their company now."

"Crap," says John.

"We will get them back," assures Vickie.

Tom smiles with a troubled look. "I am sure we will. I believe you guys." Vickie and John walk out as John asks Vickie, "I hope you have a plan." Vickie smiles. "Yes, I do." Vickie heads to her office and spends her time talking to key people in various companies known to have players of the Lazarus Game. She manages to convince some of the merit of her cause. Others create policies to avoid issues as Vickie explains that news investigations and even congressional investigations are sure to follow this game. However, most find her concerns to be trivial and ignore her.

They have several meetings with clients, who courteously tell them they will consider their proposal but soon after go with other marketing companies. Some appointments cancel altogether. One company meets with them, and after a stellar presentation, the president of that company asks, "That was a great presentation, but I am concerned about this evangelism over the Lazarus Game. I have a bit of concern that your company is focused on righting some wrong and not on the best interest of advertising for people like me. I mean, what if one day you decide something is wrong with my products or company or someone in my company and began to protest me?"

"That is not the case," Tom replies. "This game is tragedy and hurting business. It is simply not good business to play with people."

"Isn't advertising playing a game with people?"

Tom looks at Vickie as she says, "Advertising persuades people to buy things not goes in their home and governs their entire life and leaves them devastated."

"But you do go into their homes through commercials and push their buttons to buy things they don't need, which leaves them more poorer than before." The room falls silent as it is obvious this company is not going to use their services. The president stands up and says, "Look, I respect what you are doing, but fighting this game is counterintuitive to your business. It is a conflict of business interest and makes you unreliable. Sorry." He leaves as Tom sits down and stares at the table.

"I'm sorry, Tom," Vickie says, "I never meant it to be like this."

"I knew this would happen. I believe in what you are doing, Vickie, but maybe we should fight this fight when we are a little bigger."

"It is your call, Tom, it is your company." John just stares without saying a word.

"John you want to chime in on this?" asks Tom. John and Vickie stare at each other as John says, "I'm with you guys whatever you decide. I am obviously concerned for my job, but every time I look at my daughter, I think, *What can I do to make this world better for her?*"

Tom says "Let me ponder this for a while."

"Sure, Tom," says Vickie. Everyone disbands as Tom heads back to his office and closes the door. Vickie and John stare at Tom pacing and looking out his office windows.

"What do you think he will do?" asks John.

"He will do what he thinks is best for his people first then big cause second."

"You want to come over for dinner tonight? It is country fried steak night, and I know Mom would love to see you again."

"I don't know."

"C'mon, she is getting bored of berating just me."

"Okay."

———◆———

That evening Vickie arrives at John's place as Marta, John's mom, answers the door. "Vickie! Well it is good to see you again. You know I was just telling John that if he was half a man, he could have a woman like you."

Vickie smiles. "Good to see you too, Mrs. Talyor." Vickie enters and sits at the dinner table and says, "How are you, sweetie?" Becky hides her face with her hands but looks up, and Vickie is hiding her face with her hands. Becky unhides her face and smiles. Vickie smiles back. John starts putting food on the table and says, "Here it is."

"Yes, his specialty," Marta says. "Heart attack on a plate. Vickie, prayer before dinner is not required but highly recommended."

"Mom!"

"Mrs. Taylor, I am still young, got plenty of time before my arteries get clogged up."

"Yeah, arteries may take a while, but you better get a laxative after eating his gravy, otherwise, clogged will mean something else." Vickie smiles as John's face turns red with embarrassment. They all sit down as John offers a prayer. Becky bows her head, and Marta rolls her eyes around and bows hers. Vickie looks down at the table, not comfortable with the religious procedure. After the prayer, Marta says, "What's wrong, Vickie, don't like religion?" "My family was never really religious," says Vickie.

"Religion is important. My son takes it a little too far sometimes, especially with his lame dinner prayers."

"Mom!"

"Well it's true, son. You think God wants to hear your robotic simple prayer before engaging yourself in gluttony? He ain't fooled. He sits up there making bets with his angels when your cookin' is going to kill you. Then when you meet him, he will tell you how effective those dumb prayers of yours was." Vickie stares at her food trying not to smile.

"Look, Mom, would you rather I was an atheist?"

"Absolutely not. You would not know what to do if you did not have God to fear. You would fear everything else as an atheist. What do you think, Vickie? You think my son could survive as an atheist?" Vickie looks up at both of them and replies, "I think John could do well no matter what."

"Pheeew," says Marta.

"You know, they say there are no atheist in foxholes," says Vickie.

"Maybe we need to dig a few and put them in it. I know Johnny here hides in his hole most of the time."

"Mom!"

"There was one time when he was a boy that he cried because his bike had a flat tire." "That would upset most kids," says Vickie.

"Yeah, but he tried to pray that God would reinflate the tire and fix it. Like God is some kind of bike mechanic."

"I knew I would be in trouble if I came home with a flat tire."

"Yeah, you would be in trouble, but you have to face the music. That has always been your problem, no guts."

John looks down at his food. Vickie looks over at John and back at Marta. "I think John does fine. He is passionate and offers a voice of reason at the office that often offsets me."

"That is nice, but if he had any balls, he would be trying to make you interested in him."

"Mom, let's not go there again."

"Look, you have a gorgeous, smart lady sitting at your home, and the only thing you can do to impress her is cook high-fat content food? You would never find a better woman than this, and you are blowing your chance." Vickie laughs as they both look at her. "Mrs. Taylor, I am not the right girl for your son. He will find the right one someday." "Oh my God you are lesbian, aren't you?"

"No, not lesbian."

"Well that is good. I was worried that my son had already turned you into a vampire lesbian." Vickie's face turns red with humor. "Vampire lesbian, okay."

"That happened to a girlfriend, Kim."

"Mom, don't bring up Kim please."

"Why not, is it a government secret? He dated a girl named Kim one time. He liked her. All of a sudden he saw her kissing another girl at a restaurant." Vickie looks over at John, who looks humiliated. "You see, my son is the kiss of heterosexual death."

"I seriously doubt that," says Vickie.

"Really? I bet you are thinking of other women right now just sitting there next to him." Vickie smiles at Marta and stands up. John stands up in respect as Marta looks puzzled. Vickie walks over to John and passionately kisses him for a solid few minutes. John drops back in his chair, almost dizzy. Vickie walks over to her chair and sits down to pick up her fork. "You see, Mrs. Taylor, I still like men." Marta looks down at her food and back at them and starts eating. The dinner is quiet while they enjoy their food.

After dinner Marta says, "I need to head home, Vickie, would you walk me to my car?"

"Sure, Mrs. Taylor." Marta hugs and kisses Becky and hugs John. John whispers, "Mom."

"It's okay, son." John has a concerned look as Vickie and Marta walk out the door. After they leave John's home Marta says, "Thank you for humoring my antics. I try so hard to get John out of his shell. He is a grown man and needs to be more assertive."

"I understand, Mrs. Taylor, but John is doing fine. I will watch over him like you asked." "I know you will. I know you two are not right for each other. I just need him to be more honest. He likes you, but he knows you are way out his league."

"I had one I thought was the right one, but he was too much like my dad."

"That happens, dearie. Youth is wasted on the young. We get all excited about a man and marry him before we know what really need."

"I am sure it works the other way around too."

"I think the problem today is people have little attention span. In my day you did not have all these distractions. Also, there was more pressure from religion, parents, and community to keep people together. Divorce was taboo long ago. Nowadays it is as common as changing the oil in your car."

"That is true, but people should not have to be pressured by outside forces to keep them together."

"Well if those forces don't keep them together, what is going to hold them together? Sure is not love. People don't love each other all the time. You have to stay true to the institution of marriage, not love. You base marriage on love only, and you will fail. But look at me, who am I to talk."

"Wisdom has no exclusive medium to come from, it can come from anything." They arrive at Marta's vehicle as Marta says, "You are a gifted lady, Vickie. John told me you are trying to take down an evil game rich people play on poor people. Let me tell you my two cents worth. Rich people have been doing this to poor people forever. Rich people want the poor to fight over race, religion, politics—anything but the real issues. The sad truth is that people are dangerous; if they are not controlled by someone bad things can happen."

"I understand the need for order and organization, but this game is not necessary. I am afraid it will cause a revolt like the one in France."

"I doubt it. As long as people have food, toys to play with, they have no real reason to revolution."

"You may be right, Mrs. Taylor."

"Of course I'm right, I am the queen bitch."

Vickie laughs. "Good night, Mom."

Marta looks up almost with a tear. "Good night, daughter." Marta was stunned that Vickie had figured out her hidden desire for a daughter and leaves.

Vickie meets John back in his home and says, "Sorry I embarrassed you in front of your mom."

"It was my pleasure. Thank you, Vickie."

Vickie smiles. "Sure, John, see you at work. Bye–bye, Becky." John waves as Vickie leaves.

# TOM'S DILEMMA

The next day at work Tom calls Vickie and John in his office. They sit as Tom says, "I have thought of this painfully and have concluded if we pursue this offensive against the Lazarus Game, we will lose this company.

"I understand, Tom."

"Well that is not just that. I think what needs to happen, Vickie, is you need to continue to take this game down but outside the company. What I propose is to let you go on the surface but keep you on the payroll. I will provide you the resources to continue your campaign alone. The pressure will be off of us while you continue. Only the three of us, our IT guy, and HR will know. I trust these people."

"What do you think, Vickie?" asks John.

"It would mean I would not have any contact physically here anymore till it is over," concludes Vickie.

"That is right," says Tom. "We will direct deposit your checks as normal and I will provide you company card under another name that will be used for expenses. I will also provide an office under its name too for you to use. You will have phones, computers, etc. Our IT guy Mike will take care of you."

Vickie looks around. "I think this is the best thing for everyone."

"I am glad you agree. We will start with a fight that will carry over into the offices, and I will fire you. That way, if anyone is spying for Dan, they will know soon enough we are out of the game-ending business."

"We doing this now?"

"Whenever you are ready. We just need to make it convincing."

"I am ready now."

"You ready, John?" John nods yes. Tom opens the door; "Vickie, stopping this game was your idea, and it is killing us!"

"Well if you had any guts you would continue with it!"

"We can't afford for you to use our company for political reasons."

"Don't give me that, Tom, you are just a piece of chicken shit."

"Get the hell out of my office!"

"I will get out of your office, but I am not stopping till I end that damn game!" Vickie and Tom walk out into the main office area as everyone looks in shock. "Well pack your stuff, you are fired!"

"Fine!" Vickie goes to her office and starts to put her belongings into a box. John turns to Tom. "I'm sorry, Tom, I never liked her idea to stop that game anyway."

"I know, John. We don't have to play the game here, but that was not good enough for her. Let's get back to business." Vickie leaves with a pissed off look on her face as Tom gives her the same look back. As Vickie leaves, Tom calls a company meeting in the conference room. Everyone gathers as Tom says, "Look, people, I am sorry you had to witness that. Vickie is such a powerful personality as you all know that she felt she could use our company as a soapbox for her personal agendas, primarily trying to stop a corporate game that is played. Well while I don't agree with the game, I don't see it as that bad. We will just move forward without Vickie and her political agendas." Stunned, everyone walks out, slowly murmuring amongst each other. Tom later walks in John's office. "John, what is the word out there."

"I think it was completely convincing." Tom picks up John's office phone and calls the IT guy Mike in. Mike arrives, and Tom closes the door.

"I already closed out Vickie's accounts," says Mike.

"Good," Tom says. "I need to entrust you with something."

"Sure."

"I know you well and trust you. We did not really fire Vickie. We needed to stage that scene so anyone spying on us would think she left. The heat on the company is too much for her to publicly stay and fight this game here. She is going to fight it alone with our support privately."

Mike smiles. "Awesome!"

"Keep it under wraps."

"Sorry, will do."

"Good, here is what I need. I need you to monitor the phone records right after the fight and meeting. Let me know who has called anyone right after. I am looking for someone informing someone about the fight. That might be our spy. Secondly, contact Vickie on her personal phone and work with her setting up her new office. In the following days I will have the office leased under that second company I had long ago. It is not very traceable to me. Once it is set up, you get her going with phones and computers."

"Got it." Mike leaves as John says, "I hope it works."

"It will have to," says Tom.

An hour passes, and Mike goes into Tom's office. Tom motions to close his door. Mike says, "Here are the phone logs. There is one phone that called this number right after the meeting. The number is the direct number to Dan's office in his new company. What is interesting is that number has been called a number of times since Dan left."

"That sounds like our spy. Who has that phone here?"

"Cathy with layout design. But it gets better. When Dan was here, there are numerous internal calls between his phone and hers."

"Good work, Mike."

"What are you going to do about Cathy?"

"Nothing, if we do anything to her, they will know it is scam. Matter of fact, I need to you keep Cathy's equipment working fine. Don't draw any attention, but she needs to be perfectly functional to keep spying."

"Got it." Mike leaves as Tom calls John in his office. John comes in and closes the door. "The spy is Cathy."

"Cathy? Our Cathy in layout?"

"Yes, many calls between her and Dan's new job. Also there were numerous interoffice calls between them while he was here."

"Oh, wow, they are having an affair."

"Looks like it."

"Bet Vickie would like to know that since Dan has a family."

"Let's hold off on telling Vickie for the moment. But that might be useful when the time comes."

John laughs. "You sound like Vickie now."

"She does rub off on you, doesn't she? Besides, I know Vickie. She will find out soon enough."

"Yeah, my mom can't stop bragging about her."

<hr>

That night in a cheap hotel room Dan hears a knock at the door. He opens it, and Cathy walks in and closes the door. They embrace and passionately kiss. After a few minutes Dan pulls away and asks, "So give the me details about the fight." Cathy and he sit on the bed, and she says, "Oh my God. They had a meeting in Tom's office with her and John. Next thing you know she is storming out of his office and Tom and her are screaming at each other. Tom says something about this company can't afford to continue with her personal political agendas. She calls him a chicken shit, and he fires her."

Dan laughs. "That is absolutely great. She left right after that?"

"Oh yeah, packed her stuff and left. Then Tom met with John in his office and the IT guy. I guess to discuss closing her stuff out."

"Of course they did. Tom is very vigilant. He is a chicken shit like Vickie said. I knew he could not handle the pressure. We have almost blacklisted Tom's company completely."

"Now I have a job with your company when they go under."

"Absolutely, and a sign-on bonus as promised. I just need you to stay there and act normal for a while longer, to not raise suspicion. I also need you to watch things for a while because Tom is such a weasel. I am worried Vickie may intimidate him for her job again." "Sure, lover."

Dan smiles and starts unbuttoning her dress and kissing her on her neck. They stand as her dress drops. Dan slips off his clothes as she takes the rest of hers off. She reaches and grabs Dan's hand with is wedding ring on. She pulls his wedding ring off and licks it, then puts it on her finger. She says, "Tonight I am your wife, do with me as you will." Dan smiles and says, "You are my wife tonight and soon forever." He begins to make love to her as they moan in the ecstasy of lovemaking. Outside the hotel room, standing beside Dan's car, Vickie stares at their room as she holds a pamphlet of Dan's wife social organization.

# Happy Wife, Happy Life

Weeks pass as Tom is in his office telling John that several accounts have been created, and the pressure seems to be letting up on their business. "Apparently whoever is blackballing us has let up. We are getting people talking to us again."

"It is such a relief. Have you heard from Vickie?"

"I would think you would hear from her before me, but now I have not."

"Not a peep from her. Not since the firing several weeks ago." Tom intercoms Mike the IT guy to come to his office. Mike shows up. "What's up, Tom?"

"How is the new office coming?"

"The services were installed yesterday, and I hooked up the phone and computer. I just have some last-minute things I will finish after work today, and it is ready."

"Excellent. Have you heard from Vickie?"

"A few days ago she asked me to look up some e-mail addresses of people, but that is it."

"As soon as you are done, let Vickie now."

"Got it." Mike leaves as Tom and John stare at each other. "E-mail addresses?" asks John.

"It is the way things are going, everything is on e-mail these days. Snail mail will probably be a thing of the past."

"This whole Internet thing has me confused. I mean our computers are all connected together now. How do you keep people out of your stuff?"

"Not sure, but it is a concern. I am just getting used to cell phones you can easily carry in your hand now. Seems like yesterday they were ten pounds or you had to carry them in a bag." "I know, this technology thing just moves quicker and quicker it seems."

Tom laughs. "We are just old."

"Speak for yourself." They both laugh as tensions have lessened with the advent of new business coming in.

<hr>

That evening Mike is finishing up with Vickie's office as Vickie walks in. "Ms. Newsome, nice to see you again."

"Please, Mike, quit being a smartass."

Mike smiles. "Well I got your phone set up and the computer hooked up with an ISDN line to the Internet."

"Not sure what that means, but show me some things about the Internet." They sit down as Mike instructs her on how to find things on the internet. "Here are the three e-mail accounts you wanted. They are named unrelated to anything about you as requested." Mike shows her how to use the e-mail and asks, "Vickie, can I ask you a personal question?" Vickie stops and looks at him. "Sure, Mike."

"Do you think you can bring down this game?"

"That is not the problem. The problem is doing it without collateral damage to people you care about. I tend to be a broadsword in my methods, not a surgical instrument. But this will require surgery."

"Well good luck. Let me know if you need anything."

"Thank you, Mike. You are technical master." Mike leaves while watching Vickie pound away on the computer.

⸻⸻

Dan Childers arrives home late in his nice home, freshly painted from Trevor and his parent's work. His wife, Elizabeth, is busy with the many groups and associations she is involved with. Dan walks by her office and says, "Working late, honey?"

"I could ask the same thing."

Dan walks in and replies, "Honey, you know this new job has been extra busy. I am with a real company this time." Elizabeth keeps writing a paper and says, "Just remember your children need you to be around too."

"You hurt me, I am there for them." Elizabeth looks up and puts her pen to her lips. "You are not damaged, but you need to work a little less and spend more time on our kids."

"I plan to, just been held up." She looks at him. "Uh-huh. You just better keep your work and any other nocturnal activities to a minimum."

"What the hell is that supposed to mean?"

"That means be advised that if you are drinking again heavily and bar hopping, I will leave you."

Dan smiles with a red face. "Honey, I drink socially and business related."

"Just saying you better keep it under control, or all this and my kids are gone."

"Why do you threaten me? They are my kids too. You can't take them away from me." "Look I love you, but you know my family. If they think you are not living up to their standards, they can make things very hard for us."

"I know! Your family, family, family. God forbid we offend the Wrights and their almighty matriarch."

"Would you keep it down? If our kids hear you talk like that and repeat it at a family function, it could cause serious issues." Dan shakes his head yes defiantly. "I am going to get cleaned up and visit with our kids."

"Fine." Elizabeth returns to her work as Dan retires to clean up.

The next morning Dan is getting ready for work as Elizabeth asks, "Remember you are speaking at my woman's business club tonight."

"Yes, I will be there with bells on." He kisses her good-bye and leaves for his office. Shortly after he arrives in his office his phone rings, and it is Cathy. "Hey, beautiful, how are you?"

"Hey, lover, I heard this morning that Vickie is suing our company."

"That is funny, she is so delusional."

"You still going to that silly group of your wife's tonight?"

"Yeah, I have to make a marketing speech for these women. It is such a lame group; they think they are really doing something to help business."

"I will be so glad when it is just you and me."

"Me too. Just a matter of time. Anyway, let me let you go."

"Okay, lover, bye, and have a good day."

"You too, sweet cheeks." Dan leans back in his chair feeling that he has everything under control and is the ruler of his kingdom. He stares at the ceiling smiling at the paradise he has created for himself when the phone rings. "Dan Childers," he answers. The voice on the line comes on. "Mr. Childers, this is Jack the manager of Sun in the Fun Motel."

"How did you get my phone number and my name?"

"Well you left your wallet in one of our rooms last night and it had your business card in it." Dan pulls out his wallet from his pants. "That is not possible, I have my wallet right here."

"Well I don't know about that, all I know is I have a brown leather wallet with your business card in it."

"What else is in that wallet, a license?"

"No, no license, just some cash, a condom, some paper with…let's see…Women's Business Alliance Group in the pocket."

"I will be right there, okay?" Dan drives down to the motel and meets the manager. "I'm Dan."

"I thought your name all these times you rented a room here was Roger."

"Roger, yes, that is my middle name."

"I see, look, it ain't any of my business. Here is your wallet." Dan looks at the wallet, which has pictures of his wife and kids in it and the pamphlet of his wife's business group. On the back it is written "for a good time, call." Dan is extremely confused and asks Jack, "Did you find anything else in the room?"

"No, that is it."

"Thanks, sir." Dan leaves back to his office. He keeps staring at the wallet and is perplexed by where it came from. He calls Cathy. "Hey, Cathy, were you going to give me a wallet as a present?"

"Why, no. Why do you ask?"

"Damnedest thing, the motel had my name and number here at work from my business card. They found it in a wallet that has pictures of my family and wife's business group literature. I went down there and retrieved it. Tell me you did this as a joke."

"I don't know anything about it, I swear."

"All right, I believe you. You would tell me if you were unhappy with anything."

"Of course I would, I love you."

"Okay, sorry, this is just so odd."

"I would never do anything to screw you over if that is what you are implying." Dan pauses as silence befalls the call for a bit. "Sure, beautiful. I will see you tomorrow night."

"Okay, bye, love you." Dan hangs up as he keeps playing with the wallet. Finally it hits him, and he leaves the office again. He drives to Trevor's house and beats on the door. Trevor answers the door. "Mr. Childers, what are you doing here?"

"Explain this, you son of a bitch." Dan holds up the wallet.

"I did not steal any money from your wallet if that is what you are talking about."

"That is not my wallet but it has my family in it and business card. You could have easily got that stuff and put in a wallet to frame me."

"I don't know anything about that wallet, and frame you for what?" About that time Trevor's parents walk up to the door while Trevor's dad asks, "What is going on, son?"

"This white dude thinks I am setting him up with a wallet." Trevor's dad steps in front of Trevor and says,

"Look, Mr. Childers, I think you better leave our home. We don't know what you are talking about." Dan is furious, convinced he has figure out what is going on, "You better keep your son under control. He messes with me, and I will make his life a living hell and yours too."

"Get the hell off my property before I beat you off of it," says Trevor's dad.

Dan backs up. "I am warning you, stay out of my life." Dan leaves back to the office, visibly upset the rest of the business day and short with everyone that tries to talk to him.

Dan arrives at his wife's business club and sits with a smile, acting as life is perfect. Elizabeth conducts her business and says, "Ladies, before we hear from our guest speaker, my loving husband, we need to vote on a new member prospect. She came to us as an executive of marketing and would love to join. She has been a successful business executive and graduated with honors. I met with her this afternoon, and her credentials are impeccable. Do I hear a motion to have Vickie Newsome as probationary candidate to attend our meetings for member consideration?" Dan's face drops as he slowly looks up at his wife. One lady in the group shouts out, "I move that Vickie Newsome be approved as a probationary candidate." Elizabeth says, "Do I hear a second." Another woman yells, "I second it." Elizabeth states, "All those in favor say I." The ladies proclaim "I" in unison. Elizabeth states then, "All those opposed please say nay." Dan almost raises his arm and catches himself, while no one responds. Elizabeth slams a gavel on the sounder and says, "Motion to make her a candidate carries. Now please welcome my husband Dan to the podium."

Dan slowly stands up and fixes his suit. His wife walks by him and says, "Knock 'em dead, dear." He smiles and walks up to the podium. He pulls out his notes and straightens them, clearing his throat. Obviously shaken a bit from hearing the news of Vickie joining his wife's group, he musters his courage to speak clearly. "Ah, excuse me. This is unusual for me to be drawing a blank. Obviously a bad thing for a person of my position. Okay, I am ready, folks. There are three main principals in marketing." Dan proceeds with his speech as the women in his group act interested and his wife puts on a positive look. She sits like a good wife supporting her husband, appearing like every word out of his mouth is gospel. After his speech, everyone gives a clap as his wife walks up to the podium and says, "Thank you, dear. Wasn't that good, everyone? Well he definitely knows what he is talking about, and I am so proud of him. Before we dismiss is there any questions or concerns?" One lady raises her hand. "Yes, about the membership drive, have we come up with any ideas to get people's attention about our group?" Elizabeth says, "Yes, actually while meeting with Vickie she gave me a great idea." Elizabeth reaches into her purse and pulls out a wallet identical to the one at the motel Dan retrieved. "She says these cheap wallets can be bought by the hundreds for next to nothing. You put literature in them, and she suggested writing something cute on it like 'for a good time, call' on the back. We leave these wallets in different places and people will pick them up. They are all engaged to find money or whatever in it and find themselves being advertised to. They may even call us just to try to return it, in which we give them a pitch."

The ladies all look at each other impressed and smiling while one says, "That is ingenious, and this is from that new member candidate?" Elizabeth says, "Yes, it is." Another lady replies, "We need to get her in here now." Elizabeth responds, "Procedures first, but I think she will do well here." Meanwhile Dan is sweating as worry washes over him, which is replaced by fury knowing now who set him up. His mind is a torrent of thoughts about how he is going to take care of this. Sudden fear flashes his emotions as he realizes the wallet in the motel means she knows of his affair and where they meet. She is setting him up, and it must be to get him to leave the Lazarus Game. His mind the rest of the evening preoccupied all the way home as he sits up in at night trying to figure out how to get out of this mess.

# I Left My Wallet

The next morning Tom receives a call from Dan. "Tom, hey, this is Dan, how are things with you?"

"Doing well actually, how about you?"

"Great! How is the team?"

"They are cruising along well. We had to get rid of Vickie though."

"Oh, really, I am sorry to hear about that. What happened?"

"Well she got too religious over this Lazarus Game thing. It became and obsession, and it was affecting our business."

"Well I wished you would have done that while I was there."

"Yeah, that would been good, we could have sure used your talents over here."

"Well maybe I can throw you a bone once in a while."

"That would be appreciated. So what can I do you for, Dan?"

"I was just wanting to check up on you guys, I think about you at times. But now that you mention Vickie, I have a question about her."

"Sure, Dan."

"You don't have her home phone number by chance? I think she has some personal papers of mine because I remember lending them to her but can't seem to find them anywhere." Tom acknowledges and obliges Dan by giving her number. "Thanks, Tom, look, I need to run. Let's do lunch soon."

"Sure thing, Dan, good to hear from you." Tom hangs up the phone and smiles saying to himself, "Oh, Vickie, what are you up to?"

Soon after the phone call Vickie gets a call on her cell phone. "This is Vickie."

Dan replies, "Vickie, Dan. Look can we meet?"

"Sure where would like to meet?"

"How about the park near my company?"

"How about the motel on 12th street?"

Dan's anger begins to boil over. "Why the hell would you want to meet there?"

"Well isn't that where you take all your women to, or maybe just your whores." Dan is quiet for a bit while Vickie continues, "How about it, room 13 in thirty minutes."

"All right, see you there." Dan hangs up and starts shaking his fist up and down vigorously. "Damn it!" He looks up as office staff is staring at him. He straightens his tie and picks up some papers to pretend to read. Soon after he gets up and heads to the motel. He parks and goes to the manager's office. Jack comes out. "Hey, you are little early, Dan."

"Hey, Jack, I need the usual room."

"Your lady friend already has it." Jack points to the registration book, and Dan sees the name written on room 13 as Dan Roger Childers-Wright. He looks up at Jack with fury boiling over in his head and walks brisk fully to the room. He swings the door open on room 13 as Vickie is sitting on the bed. "Come on, Roger." Dan closes the door. "It is Dan, you bitch." Vickie stands up. "Now, now, be nice to me. I hold your hold future in my hands."

"You may think you have me by the balls, but I got news for you—"

"No, your girlfriend gets to hold those, and your wife gets to own them. What I have is the rest of you." Dan clenches his fist as the anger is swelling in him with a hate that is pouring through his soul like lava. "What are you going to do, Dan, hit me? Let me tell you something, you go right ahead if you want to. I beat you into this flea-infested carpet." He rocks back and forth, wanting so much to hit her. Vickie angles herself and bends her front knee slightly, ready to hurt him with a martial art move. The standoff is deafening with the only thing missing in the scene being a rolling tumbleweed. Vickie whispers, "Do it." Dan's anger begins to fade as his grip loosens, and the tension moves away from his stance. Vickie looks down and up at him as she stands down from her position. She then says, "Sit at the table." Dan looks down and around and then walks over to the table to sit in a chair. She follows and sits across from him. They stare for a while as Dan asks, "Why are you after me?" Vickie sits silently staring at him. "You're pissed because you got fired, I heard about it. You found out about me seeing someone and followed me here, right? Now you want to set me up. Look, I can get you a job at my company." Vickie is like a statue, not offering any tells. "It's the game, isn't it? You want me to help you stop it."

"Bingo."

"Look, you don't know that game is important to certain people."

"Who?"

Dan looks surprised. "I…I can't tell you."

"The Wrights."

"Lord, what do you know? They are dangerous, you have no idea."

"Dangerous to you maybe, not me."

"Everyone."

"Dan, don't try to throw me off."

"I'm not. Look, this game is important to them. I don't know why, but it is. My wife's family is nuts, they are one of the wealthiest families around."

"Afraid of losing your piece of their pie?"

"I could lose more than that. I just want to live a good life and enjoy things."

"How long do you think you can go before your wife finds out about your affair?"

"Look, I pick up women sometimes, but that does not mean anything real."

"I thought you had one, that implies a relationship."

"Okay, yes, it is one. She is special to me but just a vacation from my usual life. I know you as a woman can't understand that."

"You think women are not human too, we understand. Look, I don't care about your affair with whoever. What I care about is stopping this game. All I need to know is the who, what, when, and where." Dan looks around and at the table. "If I tell you everything, will you leave me alone? Leave my wife's business group alone and get out of our lives?"

"Yes."

Dan grabs a notebook and a pen out of the motel desk drawer and hands it to Vickie. "This is going to take a while." Dan spends the next several hours outlining the game and how it was started, who administrates it, and the mechanics of it. Vickie takes notes on all of it, and Dan says, "That is all of it."

"Who is the person that is in charge of things in your wife's family?"

"I can't talk about that. Look, you have everything about the game. That is all you need. When you bring it down, I will be free of playing it."

"Wasn't aware you were a prisoner of it."

"I admit it, I enjoy it. It is nice to feel like the big man controlling people. But it is an illusion I know. My wife's family are the real puppet masters. That is all I can tell you. If it is not enough, you will have to just destroy my life because I cannot help you further." Vickie stares at him for a few minutes. "All right, I will honor our agreement."

"Really? Thank you!"

"You know you are going to be found out by your wife eventually. She is much too smart for a moron like you to fool forever. I don't have to do anything to bring you down, you will do that yourself. What is funny is you are too stupid to realize it. You will leave here and still think you have it under control now that I am out of it."

"I hear you. You are absolutely right. I am going to turn my life around right now and be the perfect husband."

Vickie looks at him. "Market your crap to her." Vickie gets up and leaves the room. Dan puts his head down in his hands and says, "Lord, that was close." At that time his cell phone rings. "This is Dan."

Cathy replies, "Hey, honey, we good for tonight?"

"Hey, I'm sorry I meant to call you earlier. I am feeling sick and had to leave work." "You okay, lover?"

"I think it is stress. I just need to go home and sleep it off." Silence is on the phone. "Cathy, you still there? Cathy?" Cathy's voice comes from the motel room door. "Here."

"Oh my God where did you come from?"

"From the office phone. You left a message to meet you here, and what do I see? Vickie going into your room and you showing up shortly later. You two had a lot do here, two hours? You never spent two hours with me in the middle of the day. And in the same room we use, you sick bastard."

"No, she set me up, come in and let me explain it to you."

"I suppose that is why she was fixing her dress when she left and put on lipstick again." "Damn her, I am telling you she is playing me."

"Screw you, liar. I am so stupid to think that a man not honest with his wife would be honest with his mistress." Cathy storms out of the room as Dan yells, "Cathy!" He runs to the door, but she gets in her car and leaves. Dan's head is pounding, and he stops in the motel office. Jack walks up. "Two women, Roger?"

"It is Dan, never mind. You ever have one of those days, Jack?"

"My whole life is one of those days, son. I am the manager of a motel that only houses people screwing around."

"Yeah, you don't have any aspirins do you?" Jack hands him a small packet of them and says "on the house." Dan turns around to leave while Jack says, "Can I ask you something?" Dan turns and says "sure."

"I always wanted to know from one of you studs, what is it like to have more than one woman on the line?" Dan swallows his aspirin and looks around. "You know, Jack, it is a lot of work. It seems fun at first, but after a while it's hard splitting your life in sections. Simply not worth it, actually."

"Yeah, but you still do it."

"We are just fools trying to beat the clock." Dan leaves for home driving home, and his mind begins to start thinking of his kids. As he arrives in his house, he pauses and takes a deep breath. He walks in and calls out to his kids. Elizabeth says, "They are not here, Dan." Dan replies, "Where are you?"

"In the guest room." Dan turns the corner, and Elizabeth is sitting on the couch next to Cathy. "Oh, shit," he says.

"Come in and sit down, dear, we have a lot to talk about." Dan's head drops to the floor as he walks the baton death march to the chair facing his two women. He sits down as the evening does not bode well for him.

# THE FALL

Monday rolls around, and Cathy is called into Tom's office. She sits down as Tom says, "Cathy, I called you in here to let you know I am letting you go."

"But why?"

"You were in collusion with a competitor of our company, giving vital information that adversely affected the operation and revenue of our company. In consequence you are being let go, and the competing company you sold information to is being sued by us."

"I did not sell any information to any company."

"You had an extramarital affair with Dan Childers in which he promised to give you money and employment in exchange for information about our company. You are lucky I am not prosecuting you."

"I had an affair with him, but I was afraid of losing my job here if found out, and he was going to get me one there.

But it is over because I told his wife everything, and she is divorcing him now."

"That does not concern me, but the fact you were working for them instead of us does. Pack your things and leave now." Cathy jumps up mad and crying to storm out of his office. She grabs a few pictures on her desk and leaves, looking at Tom. John walks up as Tom says,, "Phase one is over."

Meanwhile in Dan's company he is called into the CEO's office. In there is also the general counsel for the company and CFO. The CEO tells Dan, "Dan, we are firing you as of this moment. We are being sued because you had a relationship with a woman in your old company, and they claim you were using her as a spy."

"Now wait a minute, I gave you information from her. You knew what I was doing the whole time."

"I have no idea what you are talking about, Mr. Childers. You are instructed to leave at once."

"You bastards are setting me up as the fall guy. You know who my in-laws are?"

The CFO speaks, "You mean soon to be ex-in-laws?"

Dan turns and looks at them one after another. "You guys are unbelievable." Dan clenches his fist and murmurs, "Goddamn Vickie."

The CEO says, "I am advising that further presence on our property is considered trespassing. Your personal items will be sent to your home." Dan looks like a wet dog with sweat. "Fine, does not matter where you send them." He walks to the door and says, "She will come for you too." Dan leaves the office quickly as everyone stares. The CEO says to the company lawyer, "Let Tom's lawyers know Dan is gone and offer the settlement."

⁓ ⁓ ⁓

A couple of weeks later Tom holds a company meeting. Tom paces around and looks at everyone. "It has been a tumultuous year so far. Things looked bleak for a while, and we had to let go of several people, but we managed to pull through. Business is up to the level it was before, and we even had a huge settlement with one of the biggest competitors. Because of this good fortune, I am bonusing everyone here. I have taken all the salaries and averaged them. I will present everyone here equally twenty-five percent of that average. Checks will be dispensed by the end of the day." Everyone erupts in clapping, and thank-yous go around the room. "You guys all deserve it. You make the company work, and we all share in it. As soon as you get your check, you are free to leave for the rest of the day." Everyone hugs each other and shakes Tom's hand as they leave happy.

Days pass as Vickie gets a call from Elizabeth. "Vickie, can we meet about your business membership with our group?"

"I'm sorry, I am tied up on other ventures and am going to have a hard time taking on another."

"Well if you could just spare a few minutes of your time I could really use your advice." "Sorry, no can do."

"I see. How about we cut the crap and get to the real point."

"I was wondering when you were."

"Fine. I know you set my ex-husband up to fall with his affair woman. I guess I owe you thanks for exposing it, but what really burns me is that you used my group to carry out your little plan. I don't like being used."

"Your husband was using you, not me."

"You know you don't know half as much as you think you do." Vickie pauses for a moment. "You knew about your husband's affair."

"That is my business, but factually I did. My family is well–connected, and we watch everything."

"I got the gist of it from Dan. You are a very powerful family and not to be messed with."

"You have no idea, woman."

"Suppose you educate me."

"What, so you can wreak havoc on more of us? I don't think so. I am just warning you to stay out of my business from now on."

"I have no intention of getting in your business anymore unless you get in my way." "Well then, I think we understand each other."

"I do have one question though."

"Yes?"

"Why did Dan marry someone like you if he could not handle it?"

"Women of power, wealth, and position attract men like him like moths to the flame. We know they burn out eventually. But they are manageable as long as they stay in our light. They serve their purpose. The man that can handle us are sometimes too dangerous to have."

"Interesting." They hang up as Vickie thinks to herself, *She is not done with me. She just wanted to see what she was up against.* Vickie begins to look into Elizabeth's family.

⸺⸺❧⸺⸺

Vickie meets with her IT guy Mike at her office. "Mike, can you find out what you can about the family of Senator Ken Wright. Dan had married into his family and to a woman named Elizabeth."

"Sure, I will find what I can."

"Be careful, these people are thorough in knowing things. Assume they already know everything about this little operation." Mike affirms her warning and moves to discover what he can. Vickie makes a call to her old friend Cindy. "Cin, what are you doing?"

"Hey, girlfriend, I am doing good. How is your job?"

"I am actually on leave from it."

"Oh my, what happened?"

"Not to worry, I am still on the payroll. I am on a special assignment."

"What assignment, looking for new ways to sell things?"

Vickie chuckles, "No. I am taking down the Lazarus Game." There is a pause for a minute as Cindy replies, "Holy crap. You are joking, right?"

Vickie says with a stern voice, "Afraid not."

"How can I help?"

"I need your expertise to explain in the media what damage this game has done to people. At the same time I would advise you to write papers on it."

"Why papers?"

"To help substantiate scientific understanding of this issue. If things go well, you will get published. Can you do that?"

"Very much so. I have more cases of people I have interviewed since the time I had talked to you."

"Perfect."

"Can I ask you a personal question?"

"Always, Cin."

"Were you ever disappointed in my lifestyle, my sexual orientation?"

Vickie takes a moment to ponder her answer. "Cindy, I have always loved you as a dear friend. The way you live your life is your business. Your lifestyle is not the way I live mine, and I do not agree with it. However it is not something I need to crusade against. There are so many things out there that are bad in the world for me to worry about this."

"I get made fun of and have mean things said about that it hurts. But what hurts me is the treatment that people do to my family and friends because of my choice."

"That will happen no matter what you choose to live as, straight or gay, religious or atheist, and even different religions. There is always someone that will oppose your viewpoint and lifestyle and be mean about it. You know me, I am kind of in the middle of the road on things. But I do not tolerate people hurting people I am close to even if I don't agree with my friend's lifestyle."

"A lot of bullies out there."

"Yes, and I am the biggest bully I know."

"Yes, you are, but you only bully bullies."

"You're funny. Look, Cindy, there will come a day when people will be more accepting of various lifestyles."

"Yes, but in your heart of hearts you would not allow people like me to make this choice."

"No, but I love you the same."

"I love you too, Vickie, and am glad you are my friend."

"Let me know what come up with. I am about to start the press release phase against this game." They end their conversation with small talk as they reminisce of the old college days.

It is late at night and Vickie is walking down a park walkway that she frequents to think about things. She walks upon a wallet sitting on the ground. She looks around as she knows that is the same type wallet she used on Dan and Elizabeth. She picks it up and opens it as a note is sticking up written upon it "turn around." Vickie looks forward as a feeling of threat comes over her, and she slowly turns around to see Dan standing behind her with a gun pointed at her. Vickie drops the wallet as she moves into a tight stance to defend herself. Dan stands with the gun shaking in his hand and tears rolling down his cheeks. Vickie stands still with her eyes locked on his eyes, but her attention is in her peripheral vision watching his body. Dan says, "You took my job, my wife, my kids, my love, my life." Vickie stands still, waiting for the right moment to move. Dan sweats and cries as he lowers his gun and turns away. "What the hell happened to my life?" He looks back at Vickie who has moved closer to him. Dan shakes his head at her and puts the gun to his head as she immediately moves and bends the gun away from his grip and drops him to his knees. Dan looks up at her as Vickie stands with his gun. "Kill me. Do it!" Vickie throws the gun into a nearby lake and walks back up to Dan. "I wished you would have killed me."

"Suicide is not the answer, Dan, you need to find your purpose again."

"What purpose? I have lost everything."

"I have lost everything before, and there is a life after."

Dan stands up and asks, "How do you survive with all that?" As they walk to a bench near the lake Vickie replies,

"Sometimes you can't lessen the pain but you can increase the tools to deal with it." They sit down and Dan stares at the ground with his elbows on his knees, combing his hair with his hands. He begins to sob as Vickie hesitantly rubs his back. Dan asks, "Why are you helping me after I just tried to kill you?"

"You were not going to kill me, you were just hurt."

"I guess I am going to jail for this now on top of everything else."

"Why?"

"Because I pulled a gun on you."

"What gun?" Dan clears his throat and looks at Vickie as she smiles. Dan begins to laugh, but the laughter turns to crying as he asks, "What do I do now, Vickie?"

"You need to deflate, first off. You need to go somewhere safe and sort out everything that has happened. Then you need to figure out what you want to do in life."

"All I ever wanted to do is marketing and have fun."

Vickie nods her head.

"I heard you lost your job too."

"No, I did not. I am working undercover."

"That fight at your office—"

"Staged. We knew your girlfriend was feeding you information. We used her to take the heat off the company so I could go rogue."

"Rogue for what purpose?"

"To end the Lazarus Game."

"You're that serious about it?"

"It is that serious."

"It is just a game."

"Is it, Dan? it caused the ruin in your life. I have a friend that is a psychologist. She has case after case of people that have killed themselves, suffered trauma and it has ruined lives."

"How can a game do this?"

"It is not just a game, it is control method. There is something much more behind it." "I don't understand."

"I don't either but am beginning to become aware of it. I suspect that your in-laws have something to do with it."

"You mean ex-in-laws, I was served with divorce papers a few days ago and a clear understanding that I had no custody with a warning to accept it."

"I am sorry for that. I have already been threatened by your ex Elizabeth about using her group to stop you. Matter of fact, she already knew about your affair."

"I loved Cathy, you know. I really did want to marry her."

"You need to focus on you and the now."

"I have no place to go, everything was in Elizabeth's name. She cut me off from our accounts. I only have the cash that I stashed for emergencies she did not know about." They sit quietly for a few minutes. "Sorry I threw your gun away," Vickie says.

"That is okay, it was a gift from Elizabeth." They both laugh for a bit. "I want you to trust me," Vickie says.

"Trust you for what?"

"I will fix things for you if you give me a chance." Dan exhales and says, "What else am I going to do?"

Trevor and his family answer a late night knock at the door. "Miss Newsome, I mean Vickie, what can I do for you?" Vickie moves aside and Dan turns toward Trevor. "What is he doing here?"

"He needs a place to hang out for a while."

Trevor's dad says, "That man accused us the last time he was here. He is not welcome." "It was not his fault, it was mine. I set him up because of things that were happening at the office. Look, I will pay you guys. Dan could use your help." Dan looks off into the distance and back at the ground. Trevor's mom steps out and walks up to Dan as he looks up into her eyes. She grabs Dan by the arm and says, "come inside."

Trevor's dad says, "Wife, what are you doing?"

She replies, "We are taking him in." Trevor's dad walks in uttering a string of words in Spanish. Trevor watches his mom and Dan go into his house and then stares back at Vickie. "Take care of him, he is important."

"Can I ask you something?" Vickie nods. "Am I part of another game now being played by you?" Vickie puts her hand on Trevor's face. "No. This time the game is in your hands." Trevor's eyes grow large. Vickie says "Take care of him, I will be back in a few days."

A few days later Vickie visits Trevor's house. Trevor invites her in as his family are all sitting at the dinner table laughing with Dan. Vickie walks up and says, "Well that is interesting." Trevor's mom prepares a place for Vickie as she sits down. Dan looks at Vickie. "Did you know Mr. Ortiz has an interesting history. His ancestor helped the Texans in the Texas revolutionary war."

"That is interesting."

Dan speaks of history and the past few days as the merriment continues. They all enjoy the remainder of their meal, and then finally Dan and Vickie walk alone to talk.

"I am feeling much better now. I think staying with the Ortiz's was what I needed right now. They are a good family, something I never had. It astonishes me they have been so generous despite the way I used them and treated Trevor."

"t is because they are at peace with their lives and have nothing to rage against. That is something we all should strive for."

"Even you?"

"I will never have peace in my life, I am afraid. Seems I am made to fight things."

"It is your destiny."

"You find religion in your stay here?"

"No, but I am beginning to see that life has many layers."

"Well are you ready to get your life back on track?"

"More than ever."

"I have a job opportunity for you."

"Really, already?"

"I spoke with Tom, your old job at our company will be reinstated, but undercover like mine for now." Dan looks around and smiles. "What do you need me to do?" Vickie smiles back. "Help me take this game down."

"Absolutely."

"Good! Let's go get your bank account setup and personal things like place to live. Here is your first paycheck to get you going."

"Can you come back tomorrow? Then we get started. I want to stay just a little longer before I get moving on my new life." Vickie looks back at Trevor's house. "See you tomorrow." Dan smiles and walks back to Trevor's home. Vickie nods as she keeps looking back at Dan going back. A warm feeling comes over her as she realizes she has done a good thing.

# P H O E N I X

A week has passed and Dan is settled into a new apartment and is working with Vickie and Mike to work on tackling the Lazarus Game's next phase. Vickie calls a meeting with the two as well as Cindy at her strategy office.

"Here are case studies by me and other medical professionals on the severity this game has caused to people," says Cindy.

"Good," replies Vickie.

"I have found some information about the Wright family's connections using the internet but not much. They have some very good defenses from hacking," Mike adds.

"I can tell you, they hire the best," says Dan.

"I wonder how much they know?" asks Vicky.

"Assume they know everything."

"Great how do you fight against that?" asks Mike.

"An enemy that feels they know everything about you is lost in their own confidence. It only matters they continue to believe in what they know. It will work against them."

Dan looks astonished. "Holy crap and all that is good, you are a scary woman, Vic."

Vickie smiles. "Glad you are on this side of things now?"

"No kidding."

"I need to deal with your ex, Elizabeth. She needs to think she is progressing against getting back at me, then I will use that expose their interests. I need to know everything you know, Dan."

"Most of what I can tell you I did in the hotel room, but that was mostly the game. Well first off she is not the one you need to worry about."

"Senator Wright?"

"Not even him, they are all puppets. They all take their cues from a committee that runs all their family affairs like a business."

"Who is in control of it?"

"I am not sure who all is on the committee. As far as who is at the top, I am not sure."

"Can you find out?"

"I have tried already, you know trying to get ahead in her family. They are tight as a drum."

"Okay, I will work on that."

"There is someone in the family that I can talk to. They were always nice to me. It is Elizabeth's sister Constance. She introduced us actually and welcomed me in."

"Sounds like a good crack to slip in. Cindy, what are your thoughts? You have been fairly quiet."

"I have the reports of the victims of this game already done and ready to press release," says Cindy.

"You think your sources will release them?" asks Vicky.

"They are medical journals in name only, they will publish anything you pay them for."

"If they are that liberal then why would legit professionals read them?" asks Dan.

"They have their purpose. The medical profession uses them to sway opinion in various directions. The media does not know the difference between them and a reputable journal. My profession has been hindered by these guys for years, so it will nice to put them to good use for once," answers Cindy.

"Dan, as you know it only matters that someone publishes something for it to be picked up elsewhere. If it is repeated enough, it becomes truth."

"I can make sure other sources pick up the news piece Cindy releases then."

"Then we have a plan for the next phase. Anyone have questions?" Everyone looks at each other, and Vickie says, "Well then, keep each other informed, and let's get to it."

Mike and Dan begin to leave as Vickie looks at Cindy, who is still sitting. "What is going on, Cindy?"

"I need your help."

Vickie sits down next to Cindy. "What is up?"

"I hate to ask, but I am at a loss on something."

"You know you can always come to me for help."

"It is not that, I am just afraid of you actually taking this on."

Vickie smiles. "I see."

Cindy looks at Vickie. "I have no choice, I need you to fix a problem for me." Vickie nods as Cindy continues, "I have been counseling a young woman in her midtwenties. She has two kids, and her husband is a terror. He is not physically abusive, but that will happen in a matter of time when the verbal and emotional abuse no longer gives him the desired effect."

"Police cannot help in this?"

"He has not made threats against her life in front of me. I have seen them a couple of times as she managed to drag him to several sessions. He is smart enough to act straight in front of me and even admit he has issues. He tells me what he things I want to hear. But he keeps her from her family and terrorizes her constantly. I have even spoken with her parents, who are beside themselves. They literally want to kill him, but they are good religious people that are at a loss. Every time they tell their daughter to leave him, he forbids them from seeing their grandkids."

"Is he cheating on her?"

"I am sure of it because he calls some girl that he claims is a friend. He owns lots of guns and plays with them as he and his wife argue. She knows she needs to leave him but keeps feeling like he will turn around."

"He won't."

"Exactly. His displaced rage and projected guilt are in full force. Can you think of anything I can do to at least get this girl to leave him for her own good and the good of their kids before he kills her?" Vickie stares at the wall leaning back in her chair as Cindy waits for her response. Vickie closes her eyes for a moment and looks at Cindy. "I will take care of it."

"Can't you just tell me what you would do?"

"This is going to require my personal attention on it."

"Good Lord, what have I unleashed? Just promise me you will take it easy."

Vickie slowly smiles as she chuckles.

# None of Your Business

The young couple that Cindy spoke about are going into a variety store as Cindy and Vickie stand watching them from a distance.

"That is Terry and his wife, Debbie, says Cindy. "They look like a cute couple and in public he acts a gentleman, but only she sees Mr. Hyde. Here is their file with details you will need. Can I ask what you have in mind to do?"

Vickie intently stares at the store. "An intervention."

"Well happy hunting." Cindy leaves as Vickie watches Terry treat Debbie. As Cindy says, he acts fine in public and helps putting the kids in the car and the purchased items away in the car. Vickie gets in her car and follows the couple as they make their way to their apartment. He gets the bags out of the car as Debbie pushes the two young kids in their cart to the apartment. As they enter, Vickie walks up to their door to listen. A few moments she hears Terry:

"You ever buy this crap again, I will smear it all over your ugly ass! You hear me!"

"Please don't we need that to help with the baby's diaper rash," Says Debbie.

"Well if you would just wipe her ass right, we would not need rash cream."

"I am sorry that our children need things and that takes away from your beer money."

"You talk to me like that again and I will leave the air conditioning off all day."

"Please, honey, don't, the kids need to be comfortable."

"Then you better keep your mouth shut and stop wasting my money." Vickie starts to walk away satisfied she knows what she is dealing with and resolved to end this madness.

---

A couple of days later Terry leaves work to stop at his favorite bar to get his favorite precoming-home drinks. The bartender says, "Hey, Terry, what is up with you today?"

"My girlfriend broke up with today," says Terry.

"That sucks."

"Yeah, she was cool." Terry takes a drink as he looks over in the seat next to him, and there sits Vickie, bright-red dress, red lipstick, and hair that is frizzy and wild. She stands out like a beacon of enchanting female light in a poorly lit bar of lonely men. Terry's eyes are wide as his brain takes in all the visual information it possibly can competing with the effects of alcohol.

"What will you have, ma'am?" asks the bartender.

"Cola please."

"You got it, ma'am."

"That is a stiff drink you ordered," says Terry.

"I don't drink alcohol even when I am sad."

"What is wrong?"

"My boyfriend left me today."

"Same thing happened to me today."

"Your boyfriend left you too?"

Terry laughs. "No, my girlfriend."

"Was she pretty?"

"Yeah, but not as pretty as you."

Vickie smiles and looks at her cola. "Thank you."

"Look, let me pay for that."

"Thank you, kind sir. It has been a long time since someone was nice to me."

"Well you just haven't met the right person." Vickie stares like a lost lamb into Terry's eyes. "Apparently not." Terry looks back at almost disbelief that his charms are working. "Terry is my name."

"Victoria." Vickie shakes hands with Terry and keeps shaking gently for a while.

"Say, you live around here?"

"Not very close, I just of kind of wandered in this area after the breakup. For some reason this bar just seemed to call me."

"It was meant to be."

"Do you believe in destiny?"

"Absolutely. Call me stupid, but I do."

"Well, stupid, I must be stupid too." Terry looks confused and angry trying to figure out if she was insulting him or playing, but her beauty and his hopes of getting with her overrides his internal anger. "Would you like to sit at one of the tables so we can talk about it in private?" Vickie leans over to him. "I would love to." Terry smiles and like a perfect gentleman escorts her to a table. Vickie and Terry make small talk about likes and dislikes and then Vickie says, "I have to confess something to you."

"Sure what is it?"

"I am married, but I want to leave my husband. I am not happy with him."

"Wow, I am sorry to hear about that."

"I am sure you think I am a bad person."

"No, not at all. Look, I have a confession too, I am married too."

"You are not happy either?"

"No. She was okay when got together but turned into a real witch soon after. She manipulates me and yells about everything."

"Oh my God, you poor guy. How do you put up with it?"

"I do it because we have a couple of kids. You have kids?"

"No, I cannot have kids because my husband hurt me in a way that I can't anymore." "That bastard, I would take care of him for you."

"You are chivalrous and a gentleman. Maybe I should have married you instead."

"I wished I would have met you long time ago." Vickie puts her hand on his as Terry stares at her hand and back at her. "I believe in destiny, there are no accidents. Do you believe that?"

"It must be meant."

"It is getting late, and I need to get back before my husband suspects something and beats me. Here is my cell phone number. Call me anytime and let's meet again."

"I will, Victoria." Terry walks her to her car and says, "I will call you tomorrow, okay?" "I will think about you all night till then." Vickie smile as she slowly backs the car away to leave. Terry looks at her number as a warm feeling washes over him of excitement.

Terry returns to his home as Debbie says, "Dinner is ready, honey." He looks down at it as his boy and daughter look up at him. "That is great." Terry goes to the bathroom as Debbie looks at the dinner in confusion at his apparent happiness, but she will take it anyway she can.

<hr>

The next day Vickie gets a call from Terry. "Hey, beautiful, what are you doing today."

"I am so glad you called, I am so sad."

"What is wrong, babe?"

"My husband told me I was a horrible person and told me that everything I do is wrong. He constantly berated me all evening. I feel like I am so useless."

"Hey, listen, you are not useless. You are an incredible person."

"I could not stop thinking about you all night. Can we meet?"

"Sounds like you need to talk about things and we need some privacy. I hope it is not too forward, but we can meet at the hotel near that bar we met last night? It will give us some privacy to discuss things."

"That is perfect, I will be there the same time as last night."

"Great, will wait in the parking lot for you." They hang up as Vickie smiles. That evening Vickie rolls up to Terry waiting for her. She gets out of the car and grabs Terry in a tight hug saying, "I am so glad to see you again." Terry feels like he is living a dream and responds, "Glad to see you too." He escorts her to the room he already has rented. They enter and sit on the bed.

"I have given it a lot of thought; I know you are the guy I want."

"Well that is quick, we barely know each other."

"It feels so right, I know this is destiny. I am going to divorce my husband and run off with you. That is if you feel the same way."

"I have deep feelings for you too." Terry reaches over to kiss Vickie as Vickie stands and says, "I want you so bad it hurts, but you are married too, and I can't mess around with a married man while I am married."

"Is it a religious thing?"

Vickie sits back down and stares into Terry's eyes. "I am sorry, it is my family's way. But if we were single, I would do things to you that men only dream about. I love sex, and I think that is the only reason my husband married me because I can't get enough sex. My feelings are so strong for you, I want to go to bed with you right now, but I would never be able to live with myself if I did that while we are both married." Terry looks very disappointed while Vickie grabs his face and turns him back to her saying, "My husband will divorce me immediately if I agree to let him off the hook money wise. I have my own job and money, which is good, I don't need his. I don't care about his stuff, I have my own. If you were to leave your wife and kids, I would hook up with you."

Terry jumps up. "Now wait a minute it is not that simple."

Vickie stands up. "Why not?"

"Well I don't know, but my kids are important to me."

"Really? I would think kids would be a pain and that you would be glad to shed them off."

"This is crazy."

Vickie slowly stands up. "Well I must have made a mistake. I thought I finally found my soulmate, the Marc Antony to my Cleopatra. I guess you were just making up things to get me in bed about your wife and family."

"Look I like you, but this is not a simple thing."

"It could be." Vickie walks to the door and opens it looking back at Terry. "I am in love with you." Vickie begins to shed a tear and leaves. Terry walks to the door and sees her getting in her car crying and driving off. Vickie drives down the road crying as it turns into hysterical laughter.

A few days later Terry arrives at his favorite bar hoping Vickie would show up. He has had a few agonizing days and has been especially hard on Debbie. He sits with his drink as the bartender says. "Hey, you know that pretty lady was here just before you arrived."

"Really, did she say anything?"

"Said she was celebrating her divorce is signed today." Terry looks around and his mind swirls with thoughts. As he pays his tab he goes to his car and calls Vickie.

"Hello?"

"Hey, it is Terry."

"What do you need?"

"Been thinking about you the last few days."

"Really?"

"Yes and about us."

"What do you mean?"

"I mean I think you are right, we were meant for each other."

Vickie begins to sniffle as if starting to cry. "I signed my divorce papers today."

"Really? You know what, I told my wife I wanted a divorce today too."

"Oh my God, I think I am going to cry."

"Weird, isn't it?"

"Not weird, it was meant. You and I were meant to be together."

"Yes, I think I am in love with you too."

"I don't want you to worry. I want you to go through with the divorce and give custody of your kids to your wife. Give her child support whatever she wants. I make really good money and will take care of us. Then we will be free, and our lives will be one for the ancients." Terry pauses for a long time as Vickie says, "What is wrong, I thought you wanted me?"

"You know what, I will do it."

"If you want you can use my divorce lawyer, he will make sure it happens quick and painless."

"Go ahead and hook me up, Cleopatra." Vickie gives him the lawyer's number and says, "Soon, my love, we will be starting our new life together, Marc Antony. As soon as your divorce goes through as planned, I will buy a new car, whatever you like."

"How did I ever get this lucky?"

"Because you are a gentleman, and people always get what they deserve."

"Okay, I have some work to do. Till tomorrow, my love."

"Love you."

Terry arrives home as Debbie has supper laid out again.

"Deb, I want a divorce."

"What!"

"Here me out." Debbie sits down on the couch and starts to cry. "We are not good together, I realize that now. You bring the bad out of me, and that is not fair to us both. I have a lawyer I talked today, and he will draw it all up for us."

"I don't understand. I did everything for you. What about that? What about our kids? I stood up for you with my family."

"It was never meant to be, we just made something out of nothing. I will leave you everything, including the kids. I have agreed in the divorce papers to pay child support. I just want out, quickly."

"You have someone, don't you?"

"Yes, and we are in love."

"Don't you love me or at least your kids?"

"I love my kids, but they need to stay with you. I don't love you though, and that can't be good for the kids."

"Oh my God, I am so destroyed. How can you do this to me?"

Iit is your fault, if you were not such a negative person all the time, I might have tolerated you better."

"If I am negative, it is because you make me that way."

"That's right, blaming me again. I can't live like this anymore, I am moving out right now."

Debbie cries and pleads, "Please don't go, please stay with me. I am sorry, I am all wrong. I will do anything you want, just stay with me. I will let do those things you like in bed every night, just don't leave."

"Listen to yourself, you are so pathetic. Don't you get it? I don't love you anymore!" Terry goes to the bedroom to pack his clothes. Debbie cries as her son says, "Mommy, are you okay."

"No, angel, I am not okay." Minutes later Terry emerges with several suitcases and puts them down. He walks over to his kids and kisses them, then looks over at Debbie as he picks up his suitcases. Debbie's face looks like a wet rag of tears as she is speechless. Terry walks out the door, leaving her for good.

⸻◦●◦⸻

As the days pass Debbie meets with Cindy and discusses the issues and that she has been served with divorce papers, giving her full custody with Terry paying child support.

"This is the best thing for you, Debbie. You are lucky because most guys would have left you high and dry."

"I guess this other woman must have been so awesome he would leave it all behind."

"no, you are the awesome one, and life has opened up to you to be happy now. Trust me, this is the best thing for you."

"You really believe that, or are you just trying to make me happy?"

"No one can be happy when their partner controls their life. Wife, husband, partner—does not matter. It has to be equal respect to have a chance at happiness. Your soon-to-be ex will never be happy, and his misery is just transferred to anyone he is with. Sign those papers and start a new life for you and your kids."

Debbie stands up. "Thank you, Miss Jones, for everything." Cindy stands up and hugs Debbie as she leaves.

⸻⸻●⸻⸻

Weeks pass as Terry and Vickie casually meet, making plans for their new life. The day finally comes when Terry invites Vickie over his apartment to surprise her. Vickie arrives and they hug as Terry says, "Look at this." He hands over papers to Vickie as she reads them. "Your divorce is final."

"Now we can start things right tonight."

"Yeah, I have been thinking about that."

"What do you say we adjourn to the bedroom?"

"Yeah, about that. I don't think I want to have sex with you."

Terry's smile moves to concern. "What are you talking about?"

"Well how can I be with a man that leaves his kids and wife for another woman, especially on just the promise of sex? What kind of man are you?"

"Okay, good one."

"I am not kidding here. You are just a bastard."

"What the hell? Don't do this to me. You realize what I have given up, what you have given up to be together?"

"I did not give up anything but a little time and maybe some dignity."

"You were not married?"

Vickie laughs. "You are such an idiot. You really think a woman like me is going to just sweep you off your feet and take you after dumping your life's baggage?"

"Then why did you do this?"

"Not sure, maybe because I did not take my brain meds before. I get confused when I don't. You see, those meds keep me from being violent, but they also make me fall in love with anyone. I quit taking them today and realized I needed to tell you the truth."

Terry has a horrified look on his face. "Oh my God!"

"Sorry if this caused too much damage in your life."

"I just left my wife and kids for you."

"Think of it this way, you are free now."

Terry stands and starts walking in a pace. "I am going to kill you for this." He furiously stands toward Vickie as she moves quickly in front of him saying, "Listen, little man. I told you I was not on my meds, which makes me violent. You want to start something, I will mop your cheap apartment floor with your butt." Terry stands shocked, but the rage is overwhelming as he shakes, wanting to hit her.

"Do it, I dare you. I am not your ex-wife, I will beat you senseless." Terry stares at her eyes as they look like they are on fire. Vickie whispers, "Come on, show me what you got." Terry slowly turns around and quickly throws a punch at Vickie. Vickie instinctively grabs his punching arm and throws him over her back, slamming him to the ground hard. The sound of wheezing and sucking wind comes from him as he is done. Vickie walks over to where he can see her. She bends down and looks at him. "Thank you, Terry, I needed that." Vickie leaves as Terry starts to slowly get up. Terry pulls himself into a chair and says to himself. "What the hell just happened?"

# Accidents Happen

Cindy meets with Vickie at her office days later.

"Thank you for what you did for Debbie. She is actually dating a nice man right now that adores her kids. Turns out they were friends before Terry muscled in on her. This new guy was happy she is single now. She even told me that her ex Terry has moved on with someone else too. He must have had another on the line already."

"Did not take them long, I guess it worked out."

"I don't even want to know what all you did to make it happen. I am just glad you did not get violent about it."

"Cin, me, violent?"

"Yeah, right. Anyway, I have done the press releases for Lazarus Game, and Dan has been getting them noticed by legit media outlets."

"That is outstanding. It will take a while for it to filter out there, but it will prepare us for the next phase. The next phase will to put pressure on political people to take action against it. They really don't have a dog in the fight, so it should not be an issue for them."

"Are you sure? I thought that Dan's ex-in-laws had a senator. Remember the one that spoke at our graduation?"

"You mean mine; you went on to a further medical degree. Anyway, there are many other politicians beside him. It will work."

"Have you heard from Dan lately? I was supposed to get something from him today, but he has not answered his cell." Vickie picks up her cell phone and calls Dan's with no answer. "Nothing, let me go and check his place." Vickie leaves and arrives at Dan's apartment to no answer. As she walks to her car her phone rings. "Is this Vickie Newsome? This is Sergeant Young with the police department, do you know Dan Childers?"

"Yes, I do, we work together."

"I am sorry to inform you that Mr. Childers has been killed in a car accident."

Vickie stops suddenly and sits down on a curb. "How, when?"

"It happened this morning on I-47. Apparently witnesses say another vehicle hit his, and he went off the overpass, killing him instantly."

"What about the other vehicle?"

"I have no information on the other vehicle as it left the scene. You were left as a point of contact on the deceased as why we are calling you. Are you the right person to notify to handle his affairs?"

"Yes, I am." The police give Vickie the relevant information as she hangs up to call her office as well as Cindy and Mike to explain what has happened. Vickie arrives at Trevor's home as Trevor and his parents answer the door. Vickie is tearful as Trevor asks, "Vickie, what is wrong?"

"Dan died in a car wreck today." Trevor and his parents hug Vickie in sadness. Vickie is invited in to discuss it with them. They console her, but she tells them that she needs to be alone and leaves.

Vickie sits on the park bench where Dan and she confronted each other during his crisis. Sitting next to her is Cindy. "Hey, stranger."

"How did you find me?"

"Dan told me this is where you turned things around for him." Vickie grabs Cindy and hugs her tightly saying, "I put him in danger."

"It was an accident, they happen."

Vickie lets go of Cindy and says, "That was no accident, he was killed. I know who and why."

"Don't be silly."

"A car pushed him off the overpass at the right time. That was no accident. I know it was part of his ex-family that did him. I am sure it had to do with his press release work on the game."

"I know you are distraught, but that is no reason to start blaming things into a conspiracy theory." Vickie hands a letter from Dan that was mailed to her just a day before the accident. Cindy reads where Dan informs Vickie a blue car has been following him everywhere lately and that he does not feel safe. He thanked her for saving him and wanted to express it in case something happened to him. Vickie shows a picture taken from traffic cameras of the accident in action. It shows a blue car slamming into Dan's.

"Oh my God, how did you get this?"

"Never mind how, I have it."

"The police are investigating this."

"Yes, but as a hit-and-run, nothing more."

"You did not cause this. This is other people doing bad things."

"I know, I really do in my mind. It just hurts in my heart."

"What are you going to do?"

"I am going to make whoever did this pay and pay hard. I need you to bow out of this program lest you get hurt too."

"Not a chance, Vickie. I am not intimidated. But may I offer a thought?"

"Sure."

"Whoever did this is obviously resourceful and ruthless. From what Dan has described, they are very smart. As bad as Dan's death is, maybe it was meant not only to silence him but distract you. Get you focused on going after them so they can lay a trap for you."

Vickie looks up at Cindy and smiles. "What if the trap is too inadequate?"

"I would not risk that."

"On second thought, we need to continue as normal as if this was an accident. We will grieve and go to the funeral as normal. I need to put a very large obituary on Dan."

"He will appreciate that."

"I want the ones that did this to all know, and maybe some will show up."

A few days later a funeral for Dan commences. In attendance are Vickie and all the workers of Tom's company Dynamic Marketing. Marketing Director John walks up to Vickie and hugs her as he arrives. He has brought his daughter and mom. John's mom hugs Vickie and says, "I am sorry, sweetie."

"Thank you, Marta—mom."

"Letting that slide today." Vickie smiles with tears at Marta. Tom hugs Vickie as Cindy arrives and grabs Vickie. Cathy, Dan's ex-girlfriend, arrives and stands on the opposite side from Vickie. She cries and looks at Vickie upset. Dan's ex-wife Elizabeth shows up with an entourage of family members including her sister Constance. Dan's ex-family seems cold and unemotional as the funeral proceedings move along. The casket sits suspended over the hole by straps ready to lower it down. The preacher asks if anyone would like to say anything. No one offers anything on his ex-family's side. Vickie speaks up. "Dan, you were exceptionally smart and gifted. Though we did not agree on many things, you were a good coworker and team player. If there is any justice in this life, it would be that what you wanted accomplished will be fulfilled. I will continue with your good work, and no one will end it." Vickie pulls from behind her a red rose and lays it on his casket. She stands straight and stares at Elizabeth as she backs up back into her position in line. Elizabeth stares back as a man in shades whispers something in her ear, and Elizabeth nods yes. The man leaves as Vickie pans the entourage, memorizing the looks of everyone. The funeral ends, and Vickie stands by the walkway to shake hands with each person leaving and to see them all up close. Cathy refuses to shake her hand and just looks disgusted while leaving. Elizabeth walks up and says, "Very nice service, Vickie."

"Thank you for coming."

"Of course, he was my husband at one time." Elizabeth has a slight smile on her face as she walks away. Various men and women pass by that came with her. Senator Wright stops and shakes Vickie's hand. "Nice to see you, been a long time."

"Senator, nice to see you." He walks by as several men follow behind him, and Constance walks up to Vickie and hands her an envelope. "Vickie, is it?"

"Yes, you must be Constance, Dan has mentioned you."

"Yes, here is a check to help with expenses."

"You did not have to, but thank you."

"Please make good use of that as soon as you can." Vickie looks confused as Constance nods and leaves. Vickie turns as the ex-in-laws all shuffle into cars and coworkers say their good-byes to Vickie. "You okay, girlfriend?" Cindy asks.

"I am fine, just going to say my final good-byes and leave."

"Okay, see you at Dynamic for the reception." Vickie smiles as she watches everyone leave. Vickie turns as she looks at the casket and says, "Rest in peace, Dan. I will make sure of it." Vickie opens the letter from Constance, and there is a check for twenty thousand dollars as well as a letter that reads: "Vickie, Dan came to me asking about our family business. I was not able to answer his questions directly, but I can to you. Call this number and leave me a message. I will meet you and discuss the things that Dan wanted." Vickie looks up and leaves to the reception.

# HIDDEN LOVE

Vickie meets with Cindy after the reception and shows her the letter from Constance. "What do you think?"

"This could be the bait for the trap."

"I don't think so, I think she is for real."

"Why would she help you, especially if they killed Dan over it?"

"Not sure, but she seems genuine."

"Be careful."

The next day Vickie calls the number on the note and leaves a message to meet at the park where Vickie and Dan had been. The time arrives and Vickie is at the park bench waiting. Constance shows up on time and sits down by Vickie. "Thank you for meeting with me."

"Thank you for coming forward. Do you have something to share?"

"Yes. Dan came to me asking specific questions about our family and members of the board of our family business."

"You mean your family."

"Yes, that is what I meant. Anyway, our family is a conglomerate that owns many other companies. We are very old and have had a stake in affairs both business wise and political. I can't tell you any more than that, but I warn you that you should just drop this."

Vickie stares quietly at Constance for a few minutes and then asks, "You're afraid of your family if you talk?"

"No, I am family by blood and safe. We have rules—very old rules—that supersede any vendettas."

"Then why not talk about them to me?"

"Because that would put you in danger. Dan did not want that. What I can tell you is if your goal is to only take down the Lazarus Game, you will be okay. Go any further, and you will face a storm you can't imagine."

"You loved Dan, didn't you?"

Constance looks shocked. "What?"

"Dan said you brought him into the family. You did not introduce him to Elizabeth but for yourself. For some reason he went for Elizabeth."

Constance looks at the ground and replies, "I loved him. Elizabeth thought he was wrong for me and that he would make a good husband for herself. I watched with envy as he was with her and had kids. He was drawn to her by her strong personality but later was not happy with her and wanted to us to leave together. I refused to defy my family, and he ended up finding some woman in his office to fall in love with. It should have been with me. I hurt him."

"Make his death mean something, help me."

Constance looks at Vickie. "Even if you knew everything, you would not have the smarts, the power, the money, or influence to stop these people. Trust me, you are star in the galaxy, and they are the gravity that controls the entire galaxy." Constance stands up, and Vickie looks up at her. "Take care of yourself." Constance leaves as Vickie leans back on the bench and folds her arms.

The next day Cindy calls Vickie, "Hey, girlfriend, you okay?"

"I am fine."

"I take it you met with Constance?"

"That I did. Turns out that she was in love with Dan, but he was stolen away from her by her sister. It is a twisted tale and one that I am not interested in pursuing right now. My focus remains on the game because it influences many people."

"Good, what do we do now?"

"I will pick up the press release push that Dan was working on and continue. Once it gets enough press and becomes a hot topic, I will move on to pressuring politicians." They end their conversation as a package arrives for Vickie at her office door. Vickie sees the package has no returnable address, and she opens it. The only thing in it is photocopies of principal people playing the Lazarus Game and the people it has exploited over time. "My God, this is the smoking gun." Vickie calls the number Constance gave her and leaves the message on its voicemail: "Thank you."

# Pawns

Vickie has hired a group of people to manage a phone bank and answer incoming press questions at her office. As the press releases roll out, it begins to attract the attention of the media. Vickie begins to start making appearances on TV stations and radio programs talking about the game. She appears on a local radio station of a popular talk radio host known as Action Jackson McKenzie. AJ, as he is known, is syndicated all over the nation. "Good morning, action listeners, this is your host of the airways and earways, Action Jackson McKenzie, and in my studio today I have Vickie Newsome. I must say you are missing out not being able to see her over the radio. She is stunning and is the executive-turned-evangelist to end a corporate game that some of you may or may not be aware of called the Lazarus Game. It's 7:05 a.m. here, and let's get right to it. So, Vickie, my understanding is this is a corporate game where they recruit people not in the corporate world and try to turn them into corporate execs."

"Well, AJ, that is what it is billed as, but not quite. These zombies, as they are called, are interned to work as slaves for corporate executives that participate in the game. They do constant meaningless tasks in hopes they get exposure into a corporate life."

"Now isn't that the fate of any college intern at any company?"

"True, but they working to a viable career path during or after college as I did at one time. The pawns in this game are poor people of little to no education that have no chance of making it in the corporate world. They are used as virtually free labor and are even pitted against each other to see what they would do to win. The corporate execs that play this game sit back and make wagers on what happens. The entry fees of the game are given to a charity in the winner's name and written off as a tax deduction for that company. Meanwhile, the pawn in the game is left hanging in the wind with no more support, and they soon realize they have no path to any real future in the corporate world."

"Hmmm, that sounds like a raw deal. Tell me, did you play this game?"

"No, not interested. It was only when I saw an individual that was the pawn in the game did I take notice."

"Says here you graduated from college only few years ago, so is it wise bucking the system so early on in your career?"

"Maybe not but there is no good time like the present."

"Well it seems to me that these pawns, as you say, just go back to the life they had before."

"Seems that way, but we have medical reports that it has caused suicides and ruined lives."

"I guess it would be hard to deal with seeing heaven for a moment and then coming back to earth."

"I think most can handle that, but it goes beyond that. Some of the pawns are treated in ways that are beyond demeaning. Even beyond them, some of the execs have had issues too." "Not sure why that would bother them."

"The pressure is so great to participate and make their pawns do things inhumane that it has wrecked marriages of execs."

"So the execs may not be the pawns but are just other pieces of the game."

"Exactly."

"So who is controlling the game?"

"Not sure specifically, but I know one family of wealth and power called the Wright family are involved."

"Wright as in Senator Wright?"

"That is right."

"I am confused why a very wealthy and famous family would be interested in a corporate wager game as this."

"I am not knowledgeable of all the merit it provides them except that it is a form of control."

"Are you afraid of them suing you over singling them out?"

"Not really, AJ, if they are willing to kill one of their own in-laws, Dan Childers, and make it look like a car accident, I am willing to expose what they did."

"What?"

"Just months ago Dan Childers, an executive who was one of the biggest participants of the Lazarus Game, became a person against the game and was with me in this fight. He was married to a woman named Elizabeth Wright who summarily had her husband ruined and then killed trying to help me."

"Uh, okay, wow. Can we keep going with this? Hey, my producer says keep going, so okay. Tell us, how do you know he was murdered?"

"Traffic camera pictures taken at the accident scene show a blue car driving him off the road. Dan had messaged me in a letter just prior to this that a blue car was tailing him everywhere. Days after the accident a blue car of this make and model was found burning by police. It had been reported stolen the day of the murder. Also, it was traced back as being owned by an individual that turns out was a pawn in the Lazarus Game. I talked to him and have his deposition done by a lawyer stating that he was made to give his car up to two men and told to report it stolen when they called him back. He was called two hours after the wreck. The men obviously used it to kill Dan and then they took it to a warehouse to store it after telling the pawn to report it stolen. After the heat died down a little because the police viewed this as a simple hit-and-run accident, they burned the car."

"Well that is a story, do you have something to back it up?"

"I have the deposition of the pawn that described the men. I also have pictures taken from the gas station they pulled into to fill the car up since the pawn apparently left it almost empty. These men showed up at Dan's funeral with Dan's ex–in-law family, which I have pictures here of from a long-distance photographer. The two men are Jack Lansing and Zane Turnball, private security officers of Elizabeth Wright, Dan's ex-wife."

"Holy moley, are we getting all this? I am here to tell you folks the guys at the gas station are the guys at the funeral pictures, and that looks like the same car in the traffic camera accident. Vickie, did you show this to police?"

"As we have been talking on the show, they have been handed this file with much more information."

"Well this is a first for me, a crime solved on my show. Do you have anything else to tell us, Vickie?"

"Dan, this was for you." Vickie gets up as AJ says, "Well good-bye, Vickie, and we are going to take a break and catch our breath."

Shortly later at the home of Elizabeth Wright police arrive. "Ms. Wright, I am detective Johnson, and I am here to serve and arrest warrant for you and your bodyguards Jack Lansing and Zane Turnball." Tears begin to roll down as she is handcuffed, and her bodyguards are placed into custody. Vickie is watching her TV as the news shows the arrests of the three in connection to Dan's murder and talks about how evidence was brought to their attention by a friend of Dan Childers. Vickie smiles as her phone rings. Vickie answers and says, "Hello?"

"Are you nuts, girlfriend?" it is Cindy on the other end.

"Could be."

"The news of this is hitting everywhere; it is on the national news. Even the senator is making a statement saying he is in shock over the whole thing. Aren't you afraid?"

"That woman and her goons were coming after me next. I just got them before they got me. Now they are exposed, and anything that happens to me or those associated with me will point back to them."

"I hope so. Girl, you are scaring me to death."

"Relax, girlfriend, I have it covered." They hang up as Vickie continues eating her popcorn watching the reports on the various news channels.

# FAME

The next day Vickie watches the news as reporters walk out of the court with Elizabeth. "Ms. Wright, you just made bail. Do you have anything to say about your pending murder case?"

"I am innocent of these charges. The police have been conned by a vindictive woman by the name of Vickie Newsome."

"What is the relationship with your ex-husband and Vickie Newsome?"

"I know they worked together, and they seemed to have a relationship of some kind from what I have heard. I divorced my ex-husband over an affair he was having with Vickie and another woman at work."

"You are saying that this Vickie and another woman were involved together with your ex?"

"I only know they were seen coming out of the same hotel rooms together, and the other woman had a falling-out with my ex when she found out about Vickie. After my divorce from him was done, he found his way to Vickie. This whole murder case is Vickie getting at me for exposing their torrid affair." The reporter turns to the camera as Elizabeth walks to her car with her lawyers. "There you heard it from Elizabeth Wright, whose uncle is Senator Wright. Her court case is set for next year, but she is now out on bail. However, her private bodyguards are still in custody pending their hearing for bail. Now back to you in the newsroom." Vickie turns the TV off and sits down drinking her hot tea. She thinks to herself, *This is not over by a long shot.*

Vickie leaves to go to the park and clear her mind. As she sits on the bench, next to her sits Dan's mistress, Cathy. "Well, if it isn't Cathy."

"You bitch, you have really screwed me over. Did you watch the news of Dan's wife?" "Ex-wife, and, yes, I did. She is grabbing at straws to get off her murder case."

"Straws? She is grabbing the whole broom! I can't work in my new job without hearing whispers now. Word has got around the office like wildfire. I am the slut mistress and possible lesbian lover to you now. What am I going to do?"

"You can help me to fight this."

"Help you? I don't want to even know you anymore."

"If you want to get clear of this, you have to fight back. Otherwise, you are going to face this conjecture until the smoke clears."

"I am not doing anything but moving. My God, how did they know about the hotel we met Dan at?"

"Elizabeth has been watching Dan for a long time now so she can control him. Just like I am sure they are watching us sitting together now."

Cathy sits up straight and looks around. "I can't stand this."

"Just leave and don't worry about it. I will handle this."

"Yeah, like you handled Dan, who is now six feet under."

"Guilt does not work on me, little mistress. Dan died with dignity as a real man, which is what he longed for. Besides, it was not really you he wanted but Elizabeth's sister Constance. When he could not have her, he found you."

"That is not true."

"It is true. I am surprised Elizabeth did not have you and Constance as bridesmaids like runner-ups to Dan just to gloat."

Cathy jumps up. "I hate you!"

"Now that is no way to talk to your alleged lover."

Cathy shakes her head. "To hell with you." Cathy storms off as Vickie stands up and yells, "Don't leave, lover! There is no Dan between us anymore!" Cathy keeps walking briskly as Vickie lowers her head as if disappointed. Off in the distance is a private investigator taking pictures and using a parabolic boom microphone recording the conversation. He plays back the recording and can only make out what Vickie has yelled to Cathy at the end. With a big smile on his face, he calls from his cell phone to Elizabeth and informs her of the new data he has collected. "Ma'am, I have photos of today of Vickie and Cathy together. You were right, they would show up together."

"Did you catch their conversation?" asks Elizabeth.

"No, I could not get close enough, but I could make out the last things that Vickie yelled to Cathy as she walked away. Get this, she said, 'Don't leave, lover,' and then yelled something about no Dan between us anymore."

"Excellent! Better than I hoped for."

"I will bring the files to your lawyer's office right now."

"Good work. Keep watching Vickie." The PI packs up his tapes and equipment and looks around. Not seeing Vickie in the park anymore, he drives off. As he leaves from behind a tree, Vickie emerges, seeing his license plate.

⸻⸻⸻❦⸻⸻⸻

Cindy meets with Vickie at Vickie's office the next day. "Thank you for coming."

"I heard about Elizabeth getting out on bail. I also heard today that her goons did not make bail."

"That means she pulled some strings to keep them in jail."

"That does not sound logical, would they roll over on her?"

"I suspect it keeps them out of the reporters' view, and she can always have them killed in jail."

"You think she has that much pull?"

"Yes."

"How come she has not done anything to you?"

"Too much press on me right now, and I don't think she is quite sure what I have on her yet. Which tells me there might be more to find out."

"What is the next play?"

"Well, on Elizabeth's front, I am playing her private investigator. Cathy looked me up in the park yesterday, and I knew that someone was there watching us, so I made it look like we were scorned lovers leaving each other in anger."

"Doesn't that help her case?"

"Yes, it does."

"Okay, I am lost now."

"Trust me."

"I have learned to wait and watch."

"On the game front, the press releases are working well, and the indictment of Elizabeth threw the issue in the forefront news wise. I got my first official inquiry from Representative Henderson wanting to know more about the game. Also, a Senator Adams is working on a panel to investigate it."

"It is going according to plan."

"Let's hope so. What I need you to do now is just live your normal life and do your job. I will be preoccupied for good time working on things."

"I understand."

"How is Lisa?"

Cindy lights up and smiles. "She is good, thank you for asking. She fully supports my endeavors with you."

"She is a good person."

"You know something funny?"

"What is that?"

"Before Dan was killed, he and I worked on this press release stuff and got into the subject of me living with another woman."

"I can only imagine."

"We got into a heated argument about my lifestyle choice, and told me that I had daddy issues."

"What did you tell him?"

"Well, instead of putting on my psychology hat and overwhelming him with my education on the matter, I decided to just keep it on a base level. Told him I was in love, and it did not matter that Lisa was a woman or a man, I am in love with the person. Dan responded that he did not agree with my lifestyle, but if it made me happy, okay."

"Dan is not a bad guy but was definitely opinionated about things. Surprise you did not cheap shot him over his affair."

"Crossed my mind, but I am glad that you have accepted me as I am."

"I could never be with another woman myself, but each to their own."

"Well thank you for being my friend."

"Of course." The two reminisce about their college days as it comes time for Cindy to leave. They hug as they know it will be a while before they meet again.

⸻⬩⬩⸻

Vickie appears on a network news show interviewing her about the game and the Elizabeth Wright case. The interviewer is respected network news anchor Andrew Compton. Andrew faces the camera and starts the show. "Tonight we are talking to Vickie Newsome, corporate executive-turned-crusader and whistle-blower to a murder investigation. Welcome, Ms. Newsome."

"Please, Vickie."

"Sure, Vickie, please call Andrew. Now first off, what is the Lazarus Game?"

"Well, Andrew, it is game of wagering among various corporate execs to exploit the poor and uneducated. The game makes fools of the pawns in the game but also the execs that play, thinking it is a simple game."

"Now we have heard on your initial radio broadcast, which is now famous everywhere, that this game has destroyed many lives."

"That is correct. We have medical findings of suicides and depressions as it creates false hopes and crashes the victim to the ground hard."

"Well we have done our own investigations and have found over thirty suicides relating to this game, and two of them were the executives participating in it. Why do you think the executives took their lives?"

"Guilt. Guilt over what they were causing. Also, they feel trapped."

"Trapped?"

"If some do not play the game, they are told they would not advance in their jobs or maybe even lose their job."

"Why would a game be that important to a company?"

"It fosters loyalty beyond job loyalty. It forces the executive to be willing to do anything that might seem immoral in other company ventures. It also creates a class division among them and the pawns. It is a form of human slavery done in the style of charity."

"According to Senator Brown, he states, and I quote, 'The Lazarus Game is a harmless game that helps underprivileged people a chance to experience what they could be and in the end it benefits charities.' What do you say to that?"

"Well that is a nice endorsement that was paid for by the Chimeman Group, which is a conglomerate for the Wright family. You look at his political contributors, and that group is at the top."

"Speaking of the Wright family, you have accused one of their prominent members, Elizabeth Wright, of murder. She has been arrested and faces trial for the murder of her ex-husband Dan Childers."

"That is correct."

"Now we are hearing accusations that you were one of two mistresses of the deceased Mr. Childers."

"He did have a mistress, but it was not me. The spin of me being one of his concubines was perpetrated by Elizabeth."

"It came to our newsroom pictures of you and this other woman named Cathy together at the same hotel, the same night and this photo of you two together at a park arguing after Mr. Childer's funeral. Our source says you yelled out for this other woman not leave and that you were lovers."

"Your source is a private investigator by the name of Don Christopher, who is a good friend of Elizabeth's bodyguard currently in jail for murder of Dan. I have with me some photos of my own. Here is one of Don meeting with Elizabeth's lawyer and her lawyer giving the package given him in the previous photo. Here is a photo of Don frequenting a massage parlor known for prostitution, which you will find was busted last night thanks to tips to the police. So what does this prove? It proves nothing, just like the photos of me and Cathy. These are things taken to discredit a person. Stick with the evidence. The facts are that Elizabeth knew Dan was having an affair with Cathy and played him for her own purposes. When she finally divorced him after it was made public, she destroyed his life in every way. I would guess the fact that Dan preferred to be with a graphic designer rather than the all-powerful Elizabeth Wright must have bruised her ego. She did not even bring their kids to his funeral, that is how vindictive this woman is. I picked Dan back up from the brink, and he devoted his life to ending this vicious Lazarus Game with me. For his reward for doing right, he was cut down by Elizabeth's goons. She was afraid he would expose the things her family is involved in."

"You are now accusing one of the most wealthiest and powerful families in this country?"

"There are always good people in every company or family. However, it only takes one to bully everyone else into their agendas. Elizabeth is that bully."

"So let's say you get this game abolished, Elizabeth is found guilty of murder and put away, what is next for you?"

"I move on and get back to my job."

"You sure there are no more fights waiting for you to take on?"

"There might be a few." The show cuts to an edit of just Andrew talking to the camera. "Vickie went into details that our producers could not air due to legal reasons involving the investigation into Elizabeth Wright. We here are fairly convinced of Vickie's resolve to ending the Lazarus Game and its ill effects. We wish her well in her endeavor."

⸻⸻◆⸻⸻

The TV turns off and Elizabeth turns to her lawyer. "What do we do now?"

"Public opinion is on her side, and that weighs heavy in court cases. It is not always about fair trials or evidence but influence."

"But she has evidence too."

"True. Every time we try to discredit her, she just takes it head-on. It is like the saying that you can't blackmail an honest person."

"What do we do?"

"What about the family?"

"In light of this, they have cut me off. They do not want to draw attention to themselves. Especially with the new acquisition they are in the middle of accomplishing. Vickie mentioning our group on air may cause some undue attention to it."

"I would suggest you lay low till your trial and continue to support your business groups and charities."

"I would if they have not asked me to step down."

"I would find something to help and try to live your 'normal' life as much as possible."

"Appears so." The lawyer leaves as Elizabeth calls her PI Don Christopher. "Don, you watch the *News Hour* show?"

"Yes, I did. Creates a problem for me."

"Who cares if you went to a whorehouse?"

"That is not the problem for me. The problem is being made famous. That is a bad thing when you are living a life of stealth."

"That was that woman's whole intent apparently, to mess you up in your job."

"I can still do my job, just have to adjust things."

"Can you do something for me?"

"Sure, ma'am."

"Do you know anyone that can work her over enough to maybe scare her?"

"You think that is wise? She is certainly to make such an attack public and link it to you. You know retaliation is a felony."

"At this point I am not sure it matters. I want her hurt."

"I will arrange it."

"Good." Elizabeth hangs up the phone and mutters to herself, "Bruise my ego. I will teach that Vickie a lesson about bruising."

# Blood Thicker than Plots

Back at Dynamic Marketing Tom meets with John, his marketing director. "Have you heard from Vickie lately?"

"Not since the reception for Dan. I did catch that news piece she was on."

"She definitely turned up the heat on that one. I fear she may getting into a dangerous place with these people."

"I know, my mom had some choice words for that interview, but then again, she seems to always have those kind of words."

Tom chuckles. "She is a unique lady."

"Unique is right, but she is Mom."

"At least business is good." They end their meeting as the work day draws to a close, and John heads home. John enters his home as his daughter runs to his arms. John's mom asks, "Did you hear from Victoria today?"

"It is Vickie, and it seems like everyone is asking that. Not a word, Mom."

"Listen, if she gets hurt by the criminals, I need you to let me know."

"What are you going to do, Mom?"

"Don't discount me, I have my ways."

"I am sure Vickie is fine. No need to worry yourself about it."

"Son, understand something about a woman like Vickie. They don't know how to stop. There is no reverse in their mind, only forward and fast. That leaves her opponents only one option, and that is to stop her."

John looks concerned and stares at the wall. "Let me get food cooking."

"Don't ignore it just because it comes from an old woman. I know what I am talking about."

"Yes, Mom." His mom looks around with a disappointed look as she goes up to the mantle of pictures. "Johnny, I am proud of you." John walks out of the kitchen with a dish towel on his shoulder and a stunned look. "Did I hear you right?" Mom turns around. "Yes, I am proud of you. You are a good father and a good man." John in amazement looks around and replies, "Well it is because you are a wonderful mother."

"Cut the crap, I was hard on you. I was afraid you would become something not respectable by others, but you are respectable. I am proud of what you have accomplished."

John smiles. "I love you, Mom. Dinner will be ready soon. Chicken good tonight for you?" Mom turns toward the pictures. "That would be fine, son." Dinner is quiet and pleasant as the evening draws to a close.

⎯⎯⎯●⎯⎯⎯

The next day the daycare worker Samantha calls John to inform him that his mom has not picked up his daughter today. John informs her he will be by to pick her up. After picking up his daughter, he goes to his mom's house. There is no answer at the door, so he uses his key to go in and finds his mom in her recliner. He tries to wake her, but she has passed away. He kneels down and cries, "Mom." His daughter, not fully understanding what is going on, knows he is sad and comforts him.

After the funeral during the reception Vickie hugs John. "I am so sorry, she was extraordinary." John looks at Vickie. "Yes, she was." John hands an envelope to Vickie marked Victoria and says, "She wanted you to have this." Vickie retrieves the envelope, and with a tear in her eye nods. The reception is quiet, and people are sharing stories as it draws to a close. Vickie makes her way home and reads the letter from John's mom. "My darling daughter Victoria, I am sorry you have to read this as I am no longer in this world. In many ways we are alike in nature, headstrong, opinionated, but caring. I know you are taking on tough and even dangerous challenges. I pity those that oppose you as you are stronger than they will ever know. But people get desperate and ruthless, you must be careful. I dreamed that you were very hurt, and it troubled me greatly. I expressed this to Johnny in order for him to warn you, but he thinks I am just crazy at times. Do be careful. Thank you for taking care of my son and my granddaughter. You are a guardian of people, which is what you are made for. You may not think it or know it, but I feel your life will have great impact on the people of this world. I love you as a daughter. Never compromise yourself, never fear, never quit on what is right. Mom." Vickie's face is drenched with tears as her heart is heavy by the loss. Yet she is invigorated by her words.

⸻⸺◆⸺⸻

Days later Cindy arrives at her work place and is meeting with a new client that has issues to discuss. His name is James, and he is a young man in his early twenties unsure where to go in life. "James, it says here in my notes that you are here to discuss your future."

"I guess so."

"No need to be shy, I am here to help. No one will know what we discuss."

"No one?"

Cindy smiles. "Yes, it is kind of a rule around here."

James relaxes a bit and says, "I don't know what I want to be. I am talented and can do many things, but every time I get a job, I want to leave it because I am not sure that is where I want to be."

"Actually, that is normal for a guy your age."

"It is?"

"Yes, it is called the pigeonhole syndrome." James looks confused as Cindy explains, "What happens is you are afraid that what you do for a living will be what you will do forever. The fact is you can change jobs and careers anytime. There is no need to fear it. However ,the good thing is you are young, and if you do what you love and find a way to make money at it, you will be happy to do that for a long time."

"That is the thing; I don't know what I want to do, seems nothing makes me happy." "You are unsettled and worried. That throws everything off."

"I tried working computers but have no experience."

"Have you thought about college or even a trade school?"

"I don't want to get into massive debt. I have no patience for books anyway."

"It is hard, I had to read a lot of books to get this job. However, it was worth it."

"I am not a reader."

"Men typically are not readers as much as women. However, even reading books of any kind helps expand your mind. Do you realize that among readers that statistics of job earnings is directly proportional to education? The more you read, even fiction, the more your mind frees up and opportunities open up."

"How can opportunities come to you just because you read a book?"

"Reality is that opportunities are all around you all the time. Books prepare you for them and help you recognize them. They put them within your grasp. It opens a whole new world for you."

"Just reading books of any kind?"

"Of any kind, right. When you recognize what is out there, then you will focus on books that gear you toward those opportunities. That will help you overcome your anxiety about what job to work. I am going to task you with reading a book. Pick one fictional book on something that you like. Read it completely through and come back and tell me what you think about it."

"Okay, I am not sure how this will help, but I will do it." They both stand up, and Cindy shakes James's hand. "Excellent, James, hope to see you soon." James leaves as Cindy meets her next client. The lady sits next to Cindy as Cindy says, "Wait a minute, haven't we met." The lady replies, "No, we have not met personally, but I was at Dan's funeral. My name is Constance Wright."

Cindy sits back with her jaw open. "You are Elizabeth's sister."

"That is correct. I am here to warn you."

"Warn me about what?"

"There is a plot to hurt Vickie."

"Plot? How, when?"

"I am not sure about the details, but it is in progress. There is a plan to hurt Vickie bad."

"Your sister is behind this?"

"Yes."

"Why come to me? Why not tell Vickie?"

"My family is not watching you, which means I can approach you."

"I will certainly warn Vickie, but is there anything you can tell me more about it?"

"Not really, I only heard in passing that the attack has been planned and people hired to do the job. I am sorry, but I fear for Vickie's safety."

"It is a concern, but they have no idea what they are walking into. I would be concerned for the attackers."

"What do you mean?"

"Vickie has black belts and is very tough."

"I am glad you are confident in her abilities, but I am afraid the people my sister has hired may be skilled too." Constance stands up. "I need to leave. Please warn her soon."

"I will and thank you." Constance smiles and leaves. Cindy gets her phone and calls Vickie.

"Hello?"

"Hey, it's me, Cindy. I just Constance in my office, and she says you are going to be attacked by henchmen of Elizabeth's."

"You have any details?"

"She did not have any other than it is soon."

"Thank you for letting me know."

"Please be careful, I know you are a badass, but Constance seems to think these are professionals."

"I am sure they will be. I have to run, are you okay?"

"I am fine, just be careful, girlfriend."

"Will do, take care."

"Good-bye."

———————

Vickie walks into Sato's martial art gym as he is instructing some new students. Sato stops the lessons and dismisses his students to welcome Vickie. "Vickie, it has been a while." Vickie bows. "Sensei." Sato motions for her sit down on the mats. As she sits, she bows once more. Sato says, "Something is troubling you."

"I have stirred a great deal of trouble among a person of means, and they have hired people to hurt me."

"You are worried about the outcome."

"I am only worried that I will hurt them bad and that it will cause legal trouble, distracting me from my mission."

"Maybe that is the purpose of this attack."

"Maybe, but I kind of goaded the person into being desperate."

"I see."

"I guess I am here for confidence and wisdom."

"A fruit falls from a tree only when it is the right time to fall. You must do things in the right time. You are trained to defeat a number of people at the same time. There can only be so many people physically able to get to you at a time before they interfere with each other. If you can defeat five people, you can defeat an army."

"Must have been how Samson defeated that army from my old children's stories."

"You only need to endurance to keep going."

Vickie stands and bows. "Thank you, Sensei Sato. I just needed to hear your voice again."

Sato stands and bows. "They will attack you at night." Vickie nods and leaves.

---

A week passes with no news, but Cindy worries each day for Vickie yet continues as normal with her life. James has returned to have another session with Cindy. "James, it is nice to see you again."

"I read a book."

"Really, that is good. What did you read?"

"I read a book about a fictional man that has goes through life wandering about what to do in his life. It was like I went in the bookstore to find a book, and this book just leaped out in front of me. I related so much to the man and what he went through."

"Did you come away with any conclusions?"

"Yes, you can't just stall in life. You have to move forward even if you don't like what you are doing. Just do something till you find what to do. That was the lesson of the book. So I went out and got a simple job working in a restaurant. My goal is work that till I find a better one."

"Very good, James, that sounds like a plan."

James stands up. "Well, I have to leave because I want to get to it."

"I am proud of you, please come back and tell me how things are going?"

"Sure will, thank you, Dr. Jones."

Cindy heads back to her desk, proud of James. It has been a long day, and before she takes a few days off she finishes up work into the evening. She locks up her office and walks alone to her car in an empty parking lot. She hears "Cindy." Cindy turns around, and four men are standing as if they came out of nowhere. Cindy gulps in fear and thinks to herself, *Oh my God.* The men slowly approached as the leader says, "How is your friend Vickie lately?" Cindy is trembling in fear as she slowly walks backward to her car, but it is very far away. "I don't know what you want from me, but I warn you, this is not a smart move."

"I think you are referring to yourself. You shouldn't keep company with such people like Vickie."

"You will all go to jail for this."

"I need you to remember this and tell Vickie that if she does not back off, you or someone else she knows will be hurt much worse."

Cindy whimpers, "My God." The men approach as Cindy is almost frozen with fear as a shout of a female voice behind the men yells, "Why don't you tell me in person!" The men look back as Vickie walks out of the night shadows. "Well, well, well. Did not plan to deal with you till later." Vickie says, "Cindy, get in your car and leave." Cindy nods in fear and begins to run to her car. The leader tells the other men, "Leave her be, we will deal with Vickie." They surround Vickie as she stands like a statue, and Cindy opens her car door but is too engrossed in the view and stands to watch. A hand grabs Cindy's shoulder as she jumps and gasps. An old Japanese man smiles at her and walks toward the men. One of the men says, "Boss, who is that?" The leader says, "What do you want, old man?" He replies, "I am here to fight." The men laugh as Cindy whispers to herself, "Sato."

One of the men walks over confidently and throws a punch at Sato as Sato strikes the man in the jaw and neck, stunning him, and grabs the man's arm as a loud crack emerges from the man's shoulder. The man yells out in pain as Sato kicks him in the ribs, sending him sliding across the ground a couple of feet. He lays motionless as Sato walks up to the men. As the leader begins to say something Vickie spins her body, hitting the leader in the face with her foot, laying him out unconscious. Sato walks up to

Vickie as the remaining two men start to back up. One man says to the other, "You take one and I will take the other." The other man says, "Which one to take?" The first man replies, "I don't know, just pick one." The second man replies, "Can't pick." Vickie and Sato step towards them as they back up again. Vickie says, "The only way you make it out of here healthy is to testify who hired you." The men look at each other. "Look, it is just a job." Vickie runs at them as one man throws a punch at her, but she grabs his arm throwing him backwards toward Sato who has got him down on his knees pressing a pressure point and twisting his arm to hold him. Vickie grabs the other man, who does not defend himself and holds his hands up. "Well, what about it?" The man says, "Whatever you say."

Sato asks the other man, "What about you?" The pinned man squeezes out a painful response, "Yes, yes, please let me go." Sato smiles and pushes him down to the ground. Police begin to arrive as Cindy had called them. The men are questioned as Vickie and Sato stand near. The police officer in charge of the scene reads them their rights and asks them who set this up. One of the men looks at Vickie and Sato. Vickie is awaiting to hear the confirmation that it was Elizabeth that set them up. The man looks at the ground and says, "It was a woman named Constance." Vickie and Cindy perk up in amazement. "What? You are lying. It was Elizabeth and most likely a private investigator named Don.

"No, ma'am, it was a blonde woman a little shorter than you named Constance." The other henchman nods at Vickie. The police tell Vickie, Sato, and Cindy, "We need to talk to you too, so stick around." The hurt men are loaded up in ambulances. Vickie and Cindy look at each other stunned as Cindy asks, "You think it is true?"

"I think we were played. What was supposed to happen here is Constance warned you to warn me to throw the attention on me. I suspected that they might try something against you for helping me as I have been watching you, especially when you work late. What I did not know is since I visited with Sensei Sato, he was watching me."

"So does that mean there is another attack planned on you from Elizabeth?"

"I think these guys were the ones that were going to eventually but first wanted to hurt someone close to me. Apparently Constance is not the angel we thought. Family sticks together."

"I don't think you are in danger anymore because this has drawn too much attention," says Sato.

Vickie agrees. "I think you are right. Maybe this was just a distraction anyway, and they were planning something else."

"I am still shaking," says Cindy.

"You all right?" asks Vickie.

"I will be okay."

The police question them and make their reports. Everyone returns home.

# THE PIECES MOVE INTO POSITION

"Mind if I join you?" Vickie asks.

Constance looks surprised. "Sure." Vickie sits down at that café table and silently looks at Constance. Constance drinks a sip of her tea and says, "What can I do for you today?"

"Was just curious why you warned me through my friend Cindy?"

"My sister was going to hurt you, and I cannot allow that."

"Why am I so blessed to have such a guardian angel over me like you?"

"I believe in what you are doing."

"You know, her henchmen tried to hurt my friend instead of me, but I happened to be there."

"I am so sorry to hear they went after her, I wished I knew that they were trying that. I understood you were the target."

"Oh I was, but first Cindy."

"My sister is so treacherous in her ways."

"Seems to be a family trait."

"What do you mean?"

"You sent those men to hurt Cindy."

"Whatever possessed you to think that?"

"Two of them that I did not beat up admitted you were the one who hired them." Constance sits quietly with a look of disgust. "But you know it did not make sense to me why you would take up your sister's cause. Then it came to me, you were not. You were setting her up. You're pissed off about Dan and sent some half-ass thugs to take me on. You thought beating up Cindy would get me going after Elizabeth even harder. These thugs would eventually seek me out, and I would defeat them and have evidence Elizabeth is after me."

"You are being ridiculous."

"Am I? Why is it that the thug described you perfectly but had no idea about Elizabeth or even her PI, Don? Elizabeth's thugs are still coming after me, but you saw an opportunity to make a mess to implicate her, didn't you? You see, I think the ones she has coming are much more professional."

"You and I have the same goals, don't we?"

"Not really. I was never after Elizabeth until it was clear to me that she was going after me."

"You have any idea what my family can do to you?"

"I am learning."

"You want to go after my sister, fine, but keep it at that level. You start going after me and her, you are going to attract unwanted attention."

"Really, like who?"

"That I will never tell you. I am not your enemy."

"No, I was just the queen on the chessboard; you tried to go after your sister's pieces."

"I am not as clever as my sister, but she hurt me so bad I can't stand it."

"Then help me to stop her."

"I crossed the line already because we are not allowed to harm family."

"Who says?"

"You don't understand, these are rules, very old rules. I can be ostracized for what I have done."

"I won't screw you over, but I am asking just for information."

"This once, and that is it."

"When will Elizabeth's crew hit me?"

"Tomorrow night at your office. They know you always work late that night. There will be five of them not including the PI who I am sure will watch to make sure it works. The five are very good at what they do."

"Your family has used them before?"

"Yes, they are ex-military, highly trained, and you will not defeat them."

"Weapons?"

"No, they never have them in case of police involvement. Besides, they won't need them for you."

"Names?"

"Don't know their names."

"Who is the head of your family?"

"I will not answer that." Constance looks around and says, "I will tell you that it is a woman of formidable intelligence and resources. You do not want to be on her radar." Vickie stares at Constance. "Anything else?"

"That will do, thank you."

Constance has a look of confusion. "You're welcome." Vickie gets up and smiles to leave. Constance watches her leave and says to herself, "Good luck."

An hour later Kurt Vans of the Chimeman Group receives a call. His secretary notifies him that Constance Wright is on the phone. Kurt answers the line. "Ms. Wright, what can I do for you today?"

Vickie replies, "Actually my name is Vickie Newsome, and I am acquainted with Constance and Elizabeth Wright. May I give you some pertinent information?"

"I am not sure who you are, but I am not amused by this rouse."

"I am here to help, interested?"

"Well you have my attention."

"Elizabeth, as I am sure you know, is facing legal problems. These legal problems are partially because of me; however, she blames me for the entire thing. I am not interested in harming your family or business interests."

"Then why the phone call?"

"To warn you that Elizabeth has hired professionals that your company uses to, let's say, change the course of history. They are supposed to beat me up tomorrow night. This will cause undue attention and may get traced back to people above Elizabeth."

"So your plan is to blackmail us?"

"No, just warn you that Elizabeth is about burn a valuable resource on an unnecessary task. Do you really want to use them for this?"

"First off, I have no idea what you are talking about, and, also, how did you know to call me?"

"You are listed on the investor group associated with Senator Wright."

"I see. I tell you what, I will let the family know your concerns, and if anyone knows anything, I am sure they will turn it over to law enforcement."

"That sounds reasonable."

"I would advise you to leave Elizabeth and us alone."

"I have no problem with that." Kurt hangs up the phone and walks to a large office. A woman with long flowing black hair, black dress with a violet pendant sits behind the desk and asks, "What is it?"

"Ma'am, we have a problem."

⸻◆⸻

Elizabeth sits reading a book as a house servant brings her a phone. "Phone, madam."

"Thank you." She picks the phone up to her ear and a voice says, "You recognize who this is?" Elizabeth becomes nervous. "Yes." The female voice on the line says, "I understand you are using our resource to handle a problem tomorrow." Elizabeth's voice cracks. "Yes."

"You will cease your activity against this person immediately, understand?"

"I understand."

"Good." The phone hangs up as Elizabeth is shaking amd dialing Don her private investigator. "Don, that project for tomorrow night, cancel it."

"They are already paid and in motion. "

"They can have the money, cancel it immediately. Take no more action against that person or anyone else associated with her okay?"

"Even surveillance?"

"Yes, everything."

"I will call them right now and cancel." Elizabeth hangs the phone up as Constance walks up. "What is the matter, sis?"

"Nothing, just my lawyer advising me on my case."

"I see." Constance starts to walk off but says to Elizabeth, "You will look good in grey or orange, whatever the prison fashion is these days."

<hr>

Vickie and Cindy meet at the park; they hug and sit down.

"You okay, Cin?"

"Still a little shaken after the events. What happens now?"

"Well I think I have stopped the real attack from happening but won't know till tomorrow."

"You better hide till it blows over."

"Can't, because if it is still on, they will just reschedule. I have to rendezvous with destiny."

"Will Sato help?"

"I will not have him there in case these guys are that good, will just have to face it alone." Cindy starts to cry and hang her head down. Vickie grabs her and holds her as Cindy says, "I don't want you hurt."

"Me neither, but this is the cost." Cindy looks at Vickie as Vickie wipes the tears from her face. "Vickie, please be careful. You are my best friend in the world."

"I thought Lisa was?"

"She is my lover and my life, but you are my closest friend."

"I will be okay." They sit and talk about common things and eventually leave. The next day Cindy is preoccupied thinking about the night to come. Meanwhile, Vickie meditates and exercises back and forth. The night creeps in like a fog at Vickie's office. She looks out her window and sees nothing. Cindy sits at home rocking back and forth with her girlfriend Lisa rubbing her back for comfort. Vickie looks over at the clock, and it is the normal time she leaves for that day of the week. She takes a deep breath and makes her way out of the office. She stands outside the office building, panning around for any signs of activity. The only thing moving a bicyclist in the background and normal traffic in the road nearby. The parking lot is empty except her car and few empty ones that usually sit out there. Vickie makes the walk to her car as if she is making a walk to the edge of a cliff. Her senses are heightened, and her attention is on full as she approaches her car. A letter is being held by her windshield wiper. She grabs it and looks around the parking lot, but there is not a soul in sight. She opens her car door, and the light from the car illuminates the letter as it reads: "It is over between us, Liz." Vickie takes a deep breath and smiles while getting into her car. As she drives off, three shadows in the distance move out of the darkness. It is Sato and two of his fellow instructors that had tested Vickie years prior. Three masters of the arts that lay in wait to deal with the threat befalling their favorite student. Sato looks at his colleagues and says, "She is safe." The two bow to Sato as the evening ends peacefully.

# Call Me Jim

Cindy gets a call from Vickie at home. "Hey, Cin."

"Lord, girlfriend, are you okay?"

"Yes a note was on my car window from Elizabeth saying that it is over."

"How did that happen?"

"Let's just say I reached someone that did not share her need for vendetta."

"Now I can sleep tonight."

"Good night, Cin."

"Good night, girlfriend." Cindy hangs up the phone as Lisa asks, "Is that a good cry or bad cry?"

"I am crying in happiness. Vickie is going to be okay."

"Thank God."

"Amen."

The next day Cindy arrives at her office in time for her first appointment of the day, James. James walks in very clean-cut and happy. "Dr. Jones, good morning."

"James, nice to see you." James sits down as Cindy opens her notebook. "So what is going on with you?"

"I have been really getting into books lately, and the more I get into, the faster it seems I go through them."

"That is the way it works, James. What have you read lately?"

"Mostly crime novels. Do you think that if I became an author anyone would read my books?"

"I would. You have a very interesting personality, I am sure you would come up with interesting material. Is that something you want to do?"

"I think so, but I'm not sure how to do this."

"Well I will tell you that it is not easy. It is like being an actor, only a few are known for their works. There are many that write books but few become popular. However some of the unknown ones later became classics. Putting your mark on the world is important, and you should not be discouraged if they don't sell very well."

"I know it will take a long time to get somewhere with it, but I'm not sure how to even start."

"The best thing I think is to get some education on writing. Writing well and conveying your thoughts are the base part of writing as I was told in my college classes."

"Thank you for that. I am thinking that I should be known as Jim rather than James, sounds more official."

"I think it is fine either way, but Jim is good if that makes you feel better." James smiles while blushing. "So let's talk about how you feel on working a regular job in the meantime."

"I am fine with anything actually because I know it is temporary till my writing career takes off."

"Well you know that is the key to getting through the humdrum of work life. Knowing you are working for a good reason like family or career advancement or to make your dreams come true is why most people make it through. You see, you were so worried about getting stuck in the foreground of your life that it was sabotaging your dreams. Now you have a goal, which makes the rest manageable now."

"What if I do get stuck in a job and never become a writer?"

"You may be stuck, as you call it, in that job, but you know what as long as you keep dreaming and writing, you will always be a writer. Mozart was not just a composer; he was also a teacher and worked other jobs. But in his heart he was always a composer; the rest just paid the rent. Get it?"

"I get it. Just want to be great."

"Nothing wrong with that goal. Just expect the best but prepare for the worse. Now you have a destination goal, all you need is a map."

"You mean a plan to get to where I want."

"Exactly."

"I have a book that helps in being a successful writer, isn't that funny?"

"Yes, it is, but this brings me to another point. The real lesson of the book is to write something that people are interested in. You bought a book on how to be a writer because the person that wrote it knew there were people out there like you. Fulfill the need and make your milestones on your way to being a successful writer."

"I see what you mean. One thing that bothers me though is there is so much already wrote out there."

Cindy smiles. "Written, written out there. Anyway don't worry about it. It is not always about what is out there but what is new. People like what is new. Why do you think they remake movies all the time? What you write will be fresh and new and make it timely to appeal to people today."

"Wow, thank you, doctor."

"My pleasure. Well our time is almost up. Is there anything you would like to address?"

"I wish I was a little older because if I was I would be asking you out."

"You are sweet, James, but I am not that much older than you."

"Oh, no, I did not mean you were old. I meant—"

Cindy interrupts, "I know what you mean. Fact is I have a life partner and am very happy. But any girl would be proud to be with you."

"Yeah, I guess."

"I am serious, especially an aspiring writer."

James smiles. "Thank you, doctor."

"Call me Cindy please."

"Okay, Cindy." James has a gleam in his eye as Cindy brushes her hair behind her ears and says, "Well it is time. Next week?"

"Absolutely."

"Give me an update on your writing and your reading."

"Will do." They get up and shake hands as James shakes her hand for a good while.

"Good-bye, James, excuse me, Jim." James smiles and leaves waving as he leaves. Cindy smiles as he leaves, and then slight concern washes over her face as she heads to her desk to make notes.

John Taylor is at home reading to his daughter when a knock at the door interrupts them. He answers the door to see Vickie standing there. "Hi, John, bad time?"

"Of course not, come on in." Vickie comes in and kneels down to see little Becky. "Hi there, Becky." Becky walks over and hugs Vickie as John smiles. Vickie sits down on the couch and asks John, "How are you doing, John?" John sits down as Becky starts play with toys on the floor. "It has been hard adjusting. Becky misses Nana, but she has been a brave girl through it all."

"That is good, she is such a cutie."

John looks down at his daughter playing. "Yeah. You know, Mom was rough acting at times, but somehow I miss it."

"I can always give it you straight."

"I don't miss it that much." Vickie smiles as John laughs. "We miss you around the office."

"I miss the marketing game myself. The good thing is my mission is making progress. It just takes so long for things to happen."

"You are certainly getting the media attention."

"I got some unwanted attention too that kind of sidetracked me."

"You know, once in a while we get phone calls from people asking different questions about you."

"I am sure that is media digging around for stories.

"That is what we were figuring. Everyone knows to stick to the script."

"Have the reports been helping at work?"

"Oh, yes, but it is not the same without you there to implement things."

"I know. Hopefully this will not take long."

"You know, I am kind of envious of you. Out there taking on this game and living a life of intrigue."

"It isn't much of a life. I really do miss the marketing thing." The two pause, watching Becky play for a bit. "John, why don't you get into the dating world?"

"Little hard with this one."

"Stop making excuses, I can watch her. You need to get back into life. Work is not life, just part of it."

"Geez, you going to be my mother now?"

"Maybe." John looks at the mantel for a bit and says, "I have a lot to get sorted out first, then I can think about such things." Vickie stands up and walks over to the mantel. She looks at John and puts her hand on the picture of his deceased wife and slams it facedown on the mantel. "What are you doing?"

"Oh, nothing just moving this old picture out of the way so you can quit hiding behind it."

"Look—"

Vickie interrupts, "You look. Life is passing you by. Let me make the excuses for you. You are still in mourning for your dead wife, your mom passing has thrown everything off, your daughter needs to stay safe from others, or maybe you are just not ready."

"Now wait a minute—"

"Sounds like you are the one waiting." John gets up and walks over to the mantel to pick his wife's picture back up, but Vickie holds it down. "You feel you can't go through it again if another woman dies on you." John looks down as Vickie says, "That is it, isn't it? I am no great example about relationships and rebuilding them, but I know you are too good of a guy to waste away without loving someone else. Vickie lets go of the picture, and John lifts it back up looking at his wife. Vickie looks at the picture and turns to John, kissing him passionately. John lets go of the picture as it falls on its face as he embraces Vickie. They pull apart after a minute and he says, "Wow."

"You see what you are missing?"

"You are missing it too, are you not?"

"Yes, but I do not have a little daughter anymore like you do. That little girl needs a mommy. Please don't deprive her of that, and don't deprive yourself of someone to cook for." John smiles as Vickie says, "There you are."

"Well I guess thanks are in order." Vickie puts her hand on the side John's face and gently kisses him on his cheek. She smiles and starts to walk toward the door but stops and kneels down and says, "Becky, you take care of your daddy, okay?" Becky smiles and gives Vickie a hug and then goes back to playing with her toys. Vickie stands up and opens the door. "Good night, John."

"Good night, Vickie." Vickie smiles and leaves, closing the door. John looks over to the mantel and picks up the picture of his wife and says, "I will never stop loving you. I hope you can forgive me." John takes the picture and puts it on the dresser drawer of Becky's. He comes back in the living room and sits on the floor next to his daughter. "Becky, do you like Miss Vickie?" Becky looks up at him and nods yes. John rubs his chin and looks up in the air, smiling a bit.

⸺⸺＊⸺⸺

The next week Cindy is at her office being visited by her life partner Lisa who has brought her a bouquet of flowers for her birthday. After they visit a bit they leave her office to the front waiting area as Cindy says, "Thank you for my flowers." The two embrace and kiss as Cindy notices James is sitting waiting for his appointment. "James, this is my partner, Lisa." James stands up and has a few roses. "Nice to meet you, ma'am. Oh, these are for you, doctor."

"Why thank you, James. Lisa, James here—excuse me, Jim—is an aspiring writer." Lisa shakes James's hand and says, "Well it is an honor to meet a writer."

James smiles. "Well I am working on it." The three chuckle as Lisa turns to Cindy. "I got to get back to work, but I will see you tonight for a nice dinner."

"I am looking forward to it," Cindy says.

Lisa looks at James. "Nice to meet you, Jim." Lisa starts to walk off, blowing a kiss to Cindy. "Later, lover." Cindy smiles and turns to James. "Well you ready to get started?"

"Sure." They go into her office, and Cindy puts his roses in the bouquet with Lisa's. Cindy turns around and sits down next to James. "Thank you for the nice flowers."

"Well they are not as nice as those others."

"It is the thought that really matters, and that was very meaningful what you did."

James smiles and is blushing. "You are welcome, doctor."

"Ah-ha."

"Cindy."

"Better." Cindy opens her notebook. "Now how are you doing?"

"Well not so good lately."

"Oh."

"I did not read any books this week, just did not feel like it."

"Did you write anything?"

"No, I could not seem to think of anything to write. Actually I got mad and hit my computer."

"I know it is frustrating, but hitting your computer is not good."

"Well I broke the screen."

"I think you are running into writer's block. You know, like how an actor gets stage fright."

"Yeah, but I don't think I have anything to write about."

"Sure you do. You just have to write about things you like. Name something you really like to do, like playing video games or basketball."

"I do like video games."

"There you go. Maybe while you are playing you can imagine a story. Sound like a plan?"

"That might work." James stares at her chair as Cindy watches him.

"What is on your mind?" James shakes his head and looks away. "Something is bothering you."

"Your girlfriend Lisa, right?"

"That's right."

"You two are in love?"

"Very much so. Does that concern you?"

"How can two women love each other like a man and a woman?"

"Very much the same way a man and a woman can. I take it that it bothers you?"

"Just does not seem natural." Cindy; "well there are animals that are same sex that have lifelong relationships."

"But we are not animals."

"Let me save you some time. I have had this conversation a number of times, including with my parents."

"Parents."

"So we have some common ground there. Look, I know it offends your beliefs, and it is your right to have an opinion. Your opinion about the way I live my life with another person my same sex is yours, and I respect it. It is as valuable as any other opinion. I only ask that you respect me as a person as I respect you as a person. Can you do that?" James nods. "Good. So let's talk about this because you need the tools to deal with people like me. You will run to many more like me in the future."

"Can I ask you a question?"

"Of course, you may ask anything."

"Did you always want a woman?"

"I had feelings of not being the same as other girls but never understood it. It wasn't till college did I find the courage to let my feelings free."

"I think it is a shame because you are so beautiful that it is wasted on another woman."

"You are funny. I am not wasted on anyone. Can I give you a little truth that maybe a little embarrassing?"

"Sure."

"I think you may be a little infatuated with me and feeling jealous." James' face turns red, and he stares wide-eyed. "It is okay, it happens. It is called transference in professional terms. Students in school sometimes crush on teachers. It is perfectly normal."

"If you were not gay and single, would you go for a guy like me?"

Cindy smiles. "I think you are a wonderful young man and have a lot to offer any girl your age."

"So the answer is no."

"Not necessarily. If I was not gay and your age as well as single, I would be proud to go out with you."

James smiles. "I guess I am just unlucky."

"I don't think so. It just means the right one has not come along yet for you. When that happens, she will be the lucky one."

"Can I have a hug?"

"I don't think that would be appropriate considering the strong feelings you have for me." James stands up and starts to leave. "James." James stops and turns around. Cindy walks over to him and puts her hand on his shoulder. "Don't take it personally. You are a wonderful man." James looks at her and puts his hand on her shoulder. He pulls her over and kisses her on the lips as she pulls away. "James, please don't, it is not appropriate."

"I am sorry, I could not resist."

"I understand, do not let it bother you. It is okay, just keep it professional, okay?" James turns back and forth moving away saying, "Sorry. I am sorry."

"It is okay, James."

James leaves while saying "sorry." He briskly walks away as Cindy watches him, concerned.

# HEARINGS AS IT IS HEARD

Months have passed, and Vickie is called into Washington to appear in Senate hearings about the Lazarus Game. It is the first major attention by government to investigate the game. Vickie approaches and sits at the desk facing a semicircle of senators sitting high above her, twelve in all. On the panel is Senator Wright, who spoke at her college graduation. He stares down at her as the room is quieted by the leading senator. Silence befalls the room as Vickie looks at the dozen looking back at her. Senator Adams starts the proceedings. "Ladies and gentlemen, we are here to listen to allegations that a game known as the Lazarus Game played by corporate executives may have detrimental effects on those it purports to help and is a cruel and unusual activity. Before we hear from Ms. Newsome, do any of my fellow senators have anything to say in this respect?

Senator Wright says, "Senator Adams, I would like to say I have met this young lady during her college graduation where she was honored with an honor never given to any graduate before her. Her academics and accomplishments were exemplary, and it would behoove us to give good weight to her in these proceedings."

"Thank you, Senator Wright. Anyone else?"

Another senator states, "I know I am a young senator but also am a businessman and have played this game. I can tell you that it involves harmless wagering between those that play it at its worse. But in the norm it is a help to those that did not go to college and have the breaks that some of us enjoyed. Also, it raised money for worthy charities. How can a game that benefits so many be so evil?"

"Thank you, senator." Senator Adams looks around the panel as his colleagues wait patiently for Vickie's testimony. "Ms. Newsome, please commence with your statement, and, after we will open up with questions." The media tightens in to make sure they have her framed for TV as Vickie starts.

"Thank you, senators, for hearing me, and thank you to those listening and watching me on TV. The Lazarus Game was started six years ago apparently of unknown origin. However, that is unimportant, what is important is what it is used for and the effects it has. It is true as the senator said it is a game of harmless wagering between executives. However, that only fuels the greed and need to push the pawns in the game, which the executives call zombies specifically. The term *zombie* refers to raising a person from the dead to become alive, hence the name of the game Lazarus. Lazarus was a biblical character that was raised from the dead. The mentality is that poor people who are recruited as interns for this game are considered dead and then made alive like executives. It is this mentality that creates the class distinction between people. Dead people are considered meaningless and have no rights, and the life given them by the executives is a gift thaat can be taken away. In order to con poor people into giving up their time and effort to play this game, they are pitched with hope that they for a fleeting moment get to live a life they never could have. If they are lucky and win the game with their sponsor executive, they can be like them in a new life. The money pooled from the game is given to a charity while the company and executive simply benefits from another tax deduction. The charities often picked are ones run by the wives of the executives. Meanwhile the pawns in this game go back with nothing except the realization they were used with no money and no chance of getting anywhere. This has caused family fights, broken relationships, and even suicides. I have a report here that lists the results of each person left in the wake of this game. There have even been executives that have been divorced and left the business world in shame over what they did to these people. Executives are pushed and encouraged to humiliate these people as much as possible in order to win the side wagers. I ask, senators, how can this be a simple game when it causes so much damage to people's lives and division among the classes in society? My hope, my wish is that we see this game for what it really is, human slavery for the humor of some. Thank you."

The room is quiet as Senator Adams asks, "Any questions from the panel?"

The young senator says, "We are all impressed with your statement, Ms. Newsome, but I think you are exploiting this game for your own reasons. I am not sure what they are, but I think it is atrocious that you waste taxpayer money and our time on something that is not an issue."

"May I address the time you played the game just before becoming senator?" Vickie says. "Your zombie ended up divorced while playing the game and in the end blames you for having to constantly running errands to which he received no money for. So how did washing your car repeatedly benefit him in learning your world?"

"Listen, I am not going to be lectured by an opportunistic woman that was fired from her last job."

"Senator, I was not fired, I have been employed by Dynamic Marketing for a long time now. The fact that you think I was fired begs the question where you got your information and why would you know that to combat me here and now? Senator Adams if I may, I would like to bring a person to testify that is a pawn of this game."

Senator Adams says, "I will permit it. Please bring him in." Trevor walks in and sits next to Vickie, giving her a small smile. Vickie whispers, "Just be yourself."

"Please state your name for the record, sir," says Senator Adams.

"Trevor Ortiz, sir."

"What is your part in this?"

"I was part of the game under Mr. Dan Childers at Vickie's—I mean Ms. Newsome's—company."

"I understand Mr. Childers is the executive that passed away recently and worked with Ms. Newsome, just to be clear."

"Yes, sir."

"Did you continue to play the game after his death?"

"No, sir, I quit before that."

"Why did you quit?"

"I no longer wanted to play it. I painted Mr. Childers' house with my parents, which was a large house by the way." The room chuckles as Trevor smiles a little and looks back up at Senator Adams.

"So you felt you were being used and were getting no benefits to the game?"

"Yes, sir."

"What were you told you would get by playing the game?"

"Mr. Senator, sir, I was told that I would get to be a junior executive if we won the game. The work I was doing helped build character to prepare for it. I was told that all college interns were treated like this, but I realized they were not always. The college interns actually did have something waiting for them."

"Were you threatened in any way?"

"Yes, sir. I was told that if I talked about the chores I had to do, I would be kicked out of the game and never get to play it again."

"Any questions from the panel?" Senator Wright stares down at Trevor as Trevor recognizes seeing him once at Dan's house visiting. No questions come from the panel as Adams looks around. "Thank you, Mr. Ortiz. Mrs. Newsome, do you have anyone else to bring forward?"

"I can bring as many as you like. I think that the point has been made well. You have the complete report that I compiled of names and depositions of many that were in the game before you. It goes into the consequences of many with statistics. I can produce any of these people here you like."

"I think this good enough for us to study, and we will reconvene say in thirty days to discuss it in private and then render our findings in a few months."

"Thank you, senators." They dismiss as the press begins to question Vickie and Trevor leaving the chambers.

Vickie meets the reporters with Trevor. A reporter asks, "Ms. Newsome, do you think this fight against the Lazarus Game will hurt you in your career?"

"Hasn't yet."

"Mr. Ortiz, are you relieved to tell your story to officials and the media?"

"I only wish that will not use people anymore like this and offer real internships with real training instead without a game to get it," responds Trevor. They fight through as reporters continue to question them. The TV turns off as Kurt the COO of Chimeman Group faces the chairwoman asking, "What do you think?" She twirls her long black hair, staring at the blank TV. "Should we be concerned about this?" She responds, "This woman did not expose my dad on the panel, so the attention may stay away from us and our new acquisition. I am going to think about this for a while. Leave it to me."

"Yes, ma'am." Kurt leaves as the chairwoman says to herself, "Vickie."

# THE RETURN

Acouple of weeks pass and Dynamic Marketing employees stand around with cups of drinks in their hands. Posters hanging up saying Welcome Back hang from the ceiling. Vickie walks in, and everyone cheers loudly as she smiles and is handed a nonalcoholic drink. Behind her is Trevor, and he is handed a drink. Tom walks up. "Welcome back, Vickie. Welcome aboard, Trevor." Trevor has been hired as assistant office manager.

"Thank you, sir," Trevor says. Vickie looks at him. "Now you get to the best parts of what you did here when you were playing the game but this time are paid for it."

"I am proud to be here." Everyone shakes Trevor's hand and welcomes him. John shakes Trevor's and Vickie's hand. "Good to see you both here again." Everyone yells to Vickie, "speech!"

"In a matter of months we will know the results of the senate hearings on the game. Because of the attention placed on it, over ninety percent of the companies have discontinued the game for good. Now I am proud to be back here full time to focus on making this company better." Everyone cheers as they raise glasses.

"I have an announcement to make as well," says Tom. "Upon Vickie's return I have decided to give Vickie the position of chief operating officer and managing partner in my company. Or should I say now, our company."

Vickie gazes in amazement at Tom. "Are you sure?"

"I am very sure. If it wasn't for your efforts, we would not be where we are. You more than deserve it." Vickie wipes away a couple of tears and says in a choking voice, "Thank you. Thank you, everyone." Trevor smiles and claps with everyone.

"Everyone in celebration of all this will receive a small bonus check today by the end of the workday as a thank-you. Trevor, you have one too because you did work here before. I have even tallied the time you were here before and included pay at the rate you have now."

"Thank you, sir. I would like to thank Mr. Childers for the friendship he showed just before his death." The room is silent as Vickie raises her glass. "To Dan." "To Dan!" Tom says. Everyone says, "To Dan." Everyone enjoys a light day of work mostly conversing with each other.

Vickie retreats to her old desk and calls Cindy at her office. "Hi, Cin, how are you?"

"I am good, how are you?"

"I am back at Dynamic. They had a surprise party to welcome me and Trevor. Tom made me a managing partner and COO."

"Oh wow, that is so awesome, girlfriend. You so deserve it. You accomplished so much for your company and I am sure soon for the corporate world in general. I always knew you would do great things."

"Thank you, Cin. It is only because of friends like you that kept me going."

"You never needed anyone. You are a marble statue. Unmovable, unshakable, and steady."

"Thank you, Cindy. Enjoy the balance of your day, and we will meet up later for dinner."

"Will do." Cindy hangs up the phone, and the receptionist buzzes her office phone. "Yes?"

"You have an old client here that would like a few minutes to talk to you, James."

"Oh, James, yes please send him in." Cindy walks to the door to open as James walks up smiling. "Hello, Jim."

"Oh, it is James." He walks by Cindy to sit in his usual chair as Cindy closes the door. "Okay, James." Cindy sits down next to him and asks, "Well it has been a long time, James, how are you?"

"I am good, working at a construction site now."

"That is good hard work. How is your reading and writing coming along?"

"Oh, I gave up on that."

"Why?"

"I have nothing to write about, and books are boring."

"No, they are not boring, you were enjoying them. I was really looking forward to what you would be writing."

"No, I accepted that I am no writer, and what I want to be is in construction. Someday I will be a contractor and builder."

Cindy goes from dismay to joy. "Well if that makes you happy, then that is the right thing for you."

"I know you think I am a failure because I did not become a writer, but I am not a failure."

"I never thought you were a failure. I see success in anything you do."

"Right."

"I am serious."

"Sure. Also I know you think I am in love with you, but I am not. I am seeing a nice girl that is awesome looking."

"Well that is very nice, James. I am happy for you."

"I am not in love with you."

"I believe you."

"Just wanted to make sure you knew for sure."

"Can I offer a moment of absolute truth between us?"

"I can handle it if you can."

"Okay. I am not buying anything you are telling me. You are spending a lot of energy trying to convince me of things that are not true."

"What?"

"I know you are not happy with your job. You are punishing yourself with what you think is a mundane job and giving up your real dreams. I think you are doing this because you are crushing on me and hurting that you can't have me. Because you can't, you are throwing away everything I encouraged you to be. Sadly you are not hurting me, only yourself. Please don't throw away your life over me."

James looks stunned. "You are the only girl that understands me."

"What about your girlfriend? Or is there one?"

"There is one, but she is not you."

"Does she like you?"

"Yes."

"Why don't you focus on her? That is a good thing."

"I don't care that you are a lesbian. Please be my girlfriend. I will make you happy and do anything for you."

"You know if you want to love me, that is okay. We cannot be together as a couple, but you can be fond of me if you want. However, if you want to do something for me, don't give up your dream of writing. Do it for me, be a writer and give your girlfriend a chance. Give yourself a chance to grow into what you want to be. You and I will be friends and continue these sessions to talk like friends do." James sits fidgeting on his shirt, looking down to the ground and back up to Cindy. "I can see you are processing a great deal. The heat fumes are almost visible over your head. Understand that you are having a problem processing the emotions. You don't know how to deal with the emotions. Let me help you. It is critical that you and I work on this."

"I will be okay." Tears water up in his eyes.

"No, it is not okay. Let me help you. Will you do that?"

"Can I come back tomorrow?"

"Of course, I will make time for you anytime you need."

"I need to go home now." James stands up as Cindy does, but she grabs his arm. "James, please know this. You are safe in this world. You have nothing to worry about. We will figure it all out together. I am your friend and care for you deeply."

"Okay." He nods his head. "Okay." Cindy grabs him and hugs him saying, "I know you are hurting. Please let me help you." They look at each other as James says, "Okay, tomorrow same time." Cindy nods her head yes but feels the pressure in her heart as she knows he is in turmoil. James walks away as Cindy stares.

⸺⸺⸺◦●◦⸺⸺⸺

The next day Cindy's administrator comes in her office. "Hi, Cindy."

"How are you, sir?"

"I have some bad news. One of your clients, James, was found dead this morning by his family. He hung himself." Cindy covers her mouth with her hand. "Oh my God." Tears roll down as Cindy then puts her face in her hands.

"I am so sorry. Take a day off, of course. Tomorrow we will talk about it. We need to file an incident report for law enforcement. But for today, just let it go."

"I have to go."

"Please go." Cindy grabs her purse and leaves. She goes to the park and sits on a bench. Shortly later, sitting next to her is Vickie. Cindy looks in disbelief she is there.

"Your boss called me and told me what happened." Cindy grabs Vickie in a hug and starts to cry out loud. "I knew he was going to kill himself."

"Shhh, I know. Some people can't be helped."

"I should have been able to help him. Why could I not help him?"

"You did everything you could, and you know that." Cindy; "I know, it just hurts."

"I know." Vickie strokes her hair as Cindy laughs. "What is so funny?"

"You are always there at my lowest moments it seems."

"I always will be." They sit in silence holding each other. Vickie follows Cindy to her home and waves her good-bye as Cindy blows a kiss to her. Cindy walks in and Lisa has come home early waiting for her and has a wonderful meal waiting. "I guess you heard too."

"Vickie called me. I am so sorry."

"I feel a little better thanks to Vickie."

"That is good. I made your favorite." Cindy looks at the table and laughs while crying. She chokingly says, "Thank you." Lisa walks over and hugs Cindy as she cries. "I love you so much."

Lisa tearfully replies, "I love you too and always will." Cindy laughs. "What is so funny?"

"You and Vickie say almost the same things to me." Lisa looks confused. "Not in that way, just the way you both put things to me."

"It is because we both understand you." Cindy smiles at Lisa as she wipes Cindy's tears from her face. "Now sit down and let's eat this good food." Cindy sits down. "This looks perfect." They both start eating as Cindy says, "You know something?"

"What is that, my love?"

"I am glad I met you. I love my life with you."

"Me too. Me too." The two enjoy their evening and eventually retire to the couch to sit next to each other and watch a good movie.

# THE MINISTER

At Dynamic Marketing Tom, John and Vickie prepare for a meeting with a televised preacher known around the world that has a megachurch called Lion Temple of Zion, or LTZ for short. However, after taking over the position, the new pastor wants to upgrade his church and services with a new marketing campaign to match the new style of services. As they sit in the meeting, the new pastor and his production personnel introduce themselves.

Pastor John Austin says, "Thank you for meeting with us on short notice. You know who I am, this is my executive producer Jane Stines and director Bob Kering. You have seen our current ads for LTZ right?"

"We have seen them and researched your church well," says Tom.

John adds, "It is nice to meet you all. I am surprised that a church would have producers and directors like a movie."

"It is a show with a full production to put on a service these days," says Pastor Austin. "You see, you have to put on a show in order to inject the message in like a shot of medicine."

"I get the purpose in the production value," says Vicky.

"I understand it too," says John. "It just seems funny because I think of church as a small building with people singing and a pastor giving a fire-and-brimstone sermon."

Pastor Austin says, "Yes, and those churches our vital to any society, they are actually the lifeblood of religion. What we do is support all of them by reaching the media-addicted people that do not normally go to church. Maybe eventually they will seek out one of the local churches."

Jane adds, "What we do is not dissimilar to what Jesus did when he did his sermons, he spoke and fed people. You think some of those people were there to hear a sermon? No, they were there because they heard they could be healed or fed. That is what we do, we feed people entertainment."

"I guess you are the one that puts it all together, Bob?" Vicky asks.

"Yes, I am the put-it-together guy," replies Bob.

"You all grew up in the same religion and somehow found each other?"

"Actually, I was hired by John last year to head up things in his new church. I actually grew up in another religion, but I appreciate what John is doing, otherwise I would have not have invested myself into his program," says Jane.

Vickie asks, "What about you, Bob, same religion?"

"Actually, I am agnostic, this is a job to me, but I do listen to the sermons."

"Interesting, very interesting."

Pastor Austin interrupts, "Look, this is like a business—more to the point, it is a business. Unfortunately, we have to live in the world today, and it requires financing to reach this many people. So I need the best in the business to put this show on for me, otherwise our church is closed. I hire the best so I can get the best results. It may seem odd having nonbelievers working for me. Some of the production crew are from various religions and even atheist, but it is a job like any other, and I pay well. Are you guys followers of LTZ or religious?"

"I am fairly agnostic," says Tom.

"I believe in God but am not very religious," says John.

Pastor Austin asks Vickie, "How about you, ma'am?"

Vickie looks around. "I believe in God, but I have a lot of doubts about how people perceive him or his ways. Many other things I simply have no idea about and no concern for."

"You see I am hiring the best—you guys—and we all believe different things, yet I am sure will succeed in this one cause. It is the reality of the world. I am curious, Ms. Newsome, what you think we have so wrong about God."

"Please, call me Vickie. It is hard for me to get it pinned down. I just think with all the different religions it occurs to me that religion is really just the perception of man to interpret what God is. In our limited understanding, how could we understand an all-knowing and all-powerful creator in his totality?"

Jane says, "Now you done it. It is sermon time."

Pastor Austin smiles at Jane and looks at Vickie. "Well, Vickie, let me put it in this fashion. To a flower, God is water and sunlight. To a fish, God is water and food. To a dog, God is food, water, and sometimes a human companion. Each living thing knows God only vaguely based on its ability to perceive the world around it. So humans have more intellectual capability then plants and animals, but we still fall so short of understanding God. The reality is that we do the best we can to understand the world around us at dust level, but God is merciful and will come the rest of the way to us. So, yes, religions are our inventions, and sometimes God intervenes to influence one or another for his purpose, but in the end, it is all about our relationship to him, whether we are a flower or a person."

The room is quiet for a while, and then Vickie says, "You are a very astute man, Pastor Austin. It is food for thought. Shall we get to working on your image?" Pastor Austin nods as his producer Jane starts. "We are facing an image problem as you mention. Since Pastor Austin has taken over from his predecessor, there has been a slight division in the organization simply because the old followers do not like the new changes. They feel the pastor is too progressive and too modern and is putting on a show more than a service. However our new numbers of members have climbed, reaching people who like this type of programming. What we need is a marketing campaign that continues to reach the new people but bridges the past and keep them in the fold. For one thing, not to put too much of a fine point on it, the old people were more reliable on tithing."

"I think one of the things finding is that new people like the entertainment but not feeling they need to pay for it because it is considered entertainment. But when you church was more service-oriented it caused a sense of guilt to give is what you are saying," said Tom.

"That is exactly the problem."

"Well, it is going to be hard to push people into giving up money in this type of production. Your revenue from nongivers is going to have to come from advertisers like any popular TV show."

"We have sold some advertising but nothing that is high revenue and that does not embarrass the service we are putting on."

Vickie adds, "I think you need to give up the fact that if you put on a show, you are going to have to sell advertising to anyone, no matter what the subject matter is. You will have to trust that people will ignore it as regular TV ads and have nothing to do with you."

"Yeah, but that disenfranchises our older following again."

"That is why you need to sell regular ads during the first part of the break because that is the attention-peaking moment of the viewer, but the last ad right before returning to your show should be a soft ad. It can even be an ad for your services to reframe the viewer's mind back into church mode." Jane and Pastor Austin look at each other as Vickie says, "The last ad will reach out to your old following. It is kind of the saying it is easier to ask forgiveness than to get permission. You are doing the 'bad' stuff in ads in the beginning of the break, but the last part is asking for forgiveness and pleading for support. You can create the impression that you need funds to be able to avoid having to use ads like this to support your church. Maybe the old and some new viewers will tithe as you say to clean up things which will never happen. The synergy plays off each other. Bad ads and people paying to stop those ads, a neverending process."

"You do remember we are a church, right?"

"Look, you think that you can only go as far as you are comfortable with and say that is still righteous? Pastor, if you were a fresh new preacher and transported to here and now and watched yourself, what would you think of yourself?"

Pastor Austin looks down at the bible he carries with him everywhere and puts his hand over it, then picks it up. "The young me would not understand any of this. But then again he would not be ready to run such a church as we have today."

"Correct, as you having a problem with what I am saying now you need to do, but the future you will have no problem with it."

"My predecessor told me that the line of what is normal moves further in front of us as we get used to it. Eventually we end up in a place far from where we should be."

"Look, I do not mean to corrupt the good, I am only providing the answer to your dilemma. You want to run a church like a Broadway show, it is going to take a balancing act like no other. Maybe this is the reason why you hire people not necessarily religious so they can do the things you don't want to get yourself dirty for." Tom and John look at each other and take a breath. Pastor Austin stares at Vickie for a long time as silence creeps in over the conference room. He then smiles; "I think we have the right people for the job. What do you think, Jane?"

Jane laughs. "I think this will work for me."

Vickie looks over to the director. "What do you think, Bob?"

Bob sits up. "I am good no matter what. I am just here to direct the show."

"I am going to pray for our success. Thank you for your insight," Pastor Austin says. The meeting breaks into silent prayer as he prays silently while Vickie and the Bob look on at each other with a half-smile.

The guests leave the meeting as Tom, John, and Vickie remain in the conference room to discuss the meeting.

Tom says, "I was not sure how the pastor there was going to take your devil like temptation of him."

Vickie replies, "you don't remember your old bible stories about Adam and Eve? I gave him a fruit to eat just like Eve did Adam. What did Adam do when God busted him? He blamed Eve and God for giving him Eve. If anything bad backlashes the pastor, he will just blame us for the running the marketing campaign and me for leading it. He is smart enough to know how to play it if it goes bad for him."

"Good Lord," says John.

"Bother you, John?"

"It just amazes me how you can influence even the top of the people in this world including a famous pastor to do it your way."

"All I do is unite what people want to actually doing it. I just remove the wall separating the two things, which is their guilt or concern."

John laughs. "Isn't that the devil's job?"

"The best trick I was ever able to do was to convince the devil I did not exist."

"That is messed up."

Tom says, "Promise me one thing, Vickie."

"What is that, Tom?"

"Promise me when you finish with this ad campaign that Pastor Austin still makes it to heaven in the next life."

Vickie chuckles. "Well let's hope that God has a sense of humor, otherwise, we all will have a lot of explaining to do."

"I am going to head to my office before lightning strikes," says John.

"Probably a good idea to go to our offices now," agrees Tom.

Vickie stands up with the guys and says, "You guys are wimps."

"Yes, I am on this subject," says John. Vickie leaves. "Ha."

Vickie returns to her office, and Trevor is adding paper to her printer. "Hello, Trevor!"

"How was your meeting, Vickie?"

"It went well, we are representing a large church now."

"That is cool. Doing God's work now?"

"Don't think it is fully what God intended, but maybe he will forgive us for it."

Trevor laughs. "Okay, whatever you say."

"How are your parents?"

"Oh, I was supposed to ask you if you wanted to have dinner with us some night, any night is fine."

"Sure tonight I am free."

"I will let them know."

"Look forward to it." Trevor leaves, and the work day progresses to the time to leave. Vickie and Trevor start to leave together as John is greeted by a lady that hugs and kisses him. The new lady says, "See you downstairs."

"Be just a few minutes," replies John. The lady leaves and Vickie says, "John, who is that?"

"That is my girlfriend, been seeing each other for a week now. She works at my daughter's daycare, and we just hit it off."

"Well I am jealous but will get over it. Proud of you, John."

"Thank you." John begins to walk away as Vickie says, "You are smart man, John, hiding her away from me for a while."

John walking away yells out, "She is a nice lady, have to give her time before meeting my mom, version two." Vickie slaps Trevor. "Let's go." Both laugh as they leave. John gathers his stuff and heads to the parking lot where his girlfriend Samantha Svetlik is waiting for him. "Hi, honey."

"Sweetie." They kiss and get in the car to leave. Vickie and Trevor watch from a distance as Vickie says, "Marta, it looks like you can be at peace now."

"What?"

"Never mind." Vickie drives off to Trevor's home. As they arrive and enter Trevor's house, his parents greet Vickie with open arms." They escort her to the dinner table as Vickie says, "Look at that spread, I love Mexican food."

Mr. Ortiz says, "We just call it food."

His wife laughs. "Stop it, Juan." Juan puts his arm around his wife. "Maria is the best cook in the world, she keeps me fat and happy." Maria laughs and pushes him away. "Sit down, old man."

"Please sit down, and let's get to the food. How was work, son?"

"Great, dad." They all sit as Maria brings a bowl of rice from the kitchen and places it on the table and sits down.

"Mrs. Ortiz, this smells wonderful," Vickie says.

"Thank you, Ms. Vickie."

"Please, just call me Vickie." Vickie begins to look at what to dish to her plate first when Juan says, "Son, you want to lead us in prayer." Vickie looks around and puts her hands on her lap and begins to bow her head with the rest of the family. "Thank you, Jesus, our Lord and the Holy Mother for our food, and may it bring us good health, amen." His parents reply, "Amen." Vickie looks around. "Amen."

Maria then says, "Don't be shy, dig in. Get it before my boys do." They start passing around food as Juan says, "Vickie, this is the way tacos are supposed to be, not that Americanized Tex-Mex food."

"Oh this looks good and smells so good."

"Hey, Dad, Vickie is going to do advertising for that huge megachurch on TV everyone talks about."

"Oh, yeah?" asks Juan.

"That's right," replies Vickie.

"We never watch it, but I have seen him on the TV as I change channels."

"Interesting, you don't stop and watch him?"

"No, we are Catholic, and his religion—well I don't know what it is—but it is not ours."

"I think they are nondenominational."

Juan makes a blowing sound. "How can you be religious and not be one of the religions? Does not make sense."

"Honey, don't start a fight at the table," says Maria.

Vickie reassures her, "No, it is okay. I think the thinking behind it is so anyone of any religion can join without feeling they are pressured into being one thing or another."

"Sounds like that church is just removing its teeth so it has no opinion about anything," says Juan.

"That may be, just maybe." They eat for a while as Vickie says, "Mrs. Ortiz, these enchiladas are awesome. Very spicy and different than any I have ate before, but I love these."

Maria replies, "They are the way I was taught to make them by my grandma. It is the old way to make them, an old family recipe."

"Your family came from Mexico at one time?"

"Our family has always been in Texas, even before it was part of the United States and was its own country," said Juan.

"It was its own country?"

"Yes, that is why the capital in Austin is like the one in Washington and has its own monument, which is actually bigger than the Washington one."

"Really? I remember Dan mentioning your family fought in the Texas war or something like that."

"You have a good memory, Vickie. Yes, my ancestors fought on the side of Texas in the Texas revolutionary war."

"Wasn't that war a land grab from Mexico?"

"Oh, boy, you stirred it up now," says Trevor.

"No, it was not a land grab," answers Juan. "It was about oppression against a dictator and being independent. It was not just white people, but Hispanic people too that wanted independence. My family helped in the fight toward the end of the war. They were given land for their service, which my grandad actually sold and moved our family up here."

"Imagine what that land might be worth now," said Vickie.

"Don't remind me, it was in a good area. But he did not want to farm. He wanted a better life for his kids, and the money for the land gave him a good start. Where we live now is home, and I am proud of it."

"Home is where you are at I guess."

"That is right. It is about family."

"Maybe someday I will get some grandkids," Maria says.

"Mom!"

Vickie laughs as Trevor is embarrassed. "Well at least your family removed a dictator."

"Yes," Juan says, "but he did leave Texas alone after losing the war and later invented chewing gum."

"Now you are telling stories."

"No, he really did, look it up."

"Okay."

"You have any man in your life?" asks Maria.

"I did have a boyfriend in college, but he was too unstable, and tragedy just seemed to follow him. Well it did for me too for that matter. Maybe that was why I liked him so much. He was a lot like my dad."

"Well they say we marry our fathers."

"I am nothing like your dad," says Juan.

Maria laughs at Juan and looks back at Vickie. "My dad used to reply to things just like that." Juan looks at Maria with a disgusted look but says to Vickie, "So no man in your life or kids on the horizon?"

"I have a child, but not by my boyfriend."

"Oh."

Vickie looks up and smiles. "I was a teenager."

"You see, son, I warned you long ago about playing around," says Juan.

"No, it was not like that. I was raped by my cousin."

"Oh, dear, I am sorry," says Maria.

"It is okay; it was a long time ago." The Ortiz family are staring at Vickie as she has their full attention now. "He drugged me when I was very young and raped me. I was a wreck emotionally over it, and my mom forced me to give up my child for adoption."

"You get to see your baby?" asks Maria.

"Only for a brief few minutes, and then it was taken away. It was adopted out before it was born."

"It?"

Vickie stares at her food and moves her food around a bit with her fork. "She. It was a girl."

"You ever try to find her?" asks Juan.

Maria looks at Juan. "Dear!"

Vickie looks up. "No, it is okay. No, I did not try to find her. She would be a preteen by now. Sometimes I feel like I can feel her out there. Sounds crazy, I know."

"Not at all, I believe in such things. It is God's way of keeping us together."

"That is a nice sentiment. I don't know what I would do if I ever met her. I am terrified at the prospect of meeting her and having to explain why I gave her up."

"You were made to give her up."

"I could have fought for her."

"No, you couldn't. Believe me, as a mother too, you are not in any shape to make decisions after having a child. You are stressed, tired, and disoriented."

"Yeah."

"It is true. You will see her again, I have faith in it."

"I don't know. Like I say, I would not know what to say to her."

"How about 'I love you, daughter'?"

"I keep thinking she will want to know why I gave her up."

"Yes, she will, but she deserves to know it. My mom and I had a bond that could not be broken no matter how mad we were at each other. You will find that bond is there with yours. She will forgive you and love you no matter what."

"I wish I had your strength and confidence."

"Like my mother used to say, 'relationships are harder than anything in the world'."

"You have to have faith," agreed Juan. "I know to a person like you it seems like nothing, but faith prepares you for God's gifts. When he gives it to you, it will happen usually in circumstances you never thought it would."

"Well I admire you guys, and this family experience is such a warm thing that I have lacked so much."

"You are always welcome here," Maria says.

"Yeah, come here anytime," agrees Trevor.

"Thank you so much for the wonderful food and conversation." The evening ends as Vickie begins to leave. They all hug her as she says her good-byes. As Vickie leaves to her car, an idea goes off like a lightbulb about Pastor Austin's campaign. She begins to laugh as she opens the car door and says to herself, *Maybe that is divinely inspired.* Driving home she formulates the details of her new idea for his campaign.

# Sam Can

John is fixing his famous lasagna while his daughter Becky is playing on the floor. There is a knock at the door, and Becky jumps up and runs to the door to lightly hit it repeatedly, wanting Dad to open it. John goes to the door. "You know who that is, cutie, don't you?" His daughter looks up and keeps tapping the door. John opens the door, and Samantha is waiting with a big smile as she and John kiss. She picks up Becky. "How is my favorite little girl?" Samantha tickles Becky as the little girl laughs and giggles hysterically as she walks into John's home. John smiles and closes the door. "I have some food to finish, give me a few minutes."

"Oh I think we will be fine." She puts Becky on the floor and sits next to her. "What are you playing?" Becky picks up a little truck and shows it to Samantha with a smile on her face. "You have a truck. That is a pretty truck." Becky shows other little toy cars as Samantha shows her what the various parts of the car are called. John breaks from cooking to watch them interact. A warm feeling pours over him watching the gentle nature Samantha has with Becky. A few minutes later John puts the salad down and says, "Dinner is ready." Samantha walks to the dining table carrying Becky and places her gently into the chair to eat. She gets ready to dish out some food, and John says, "No, no, no. Just sit; I am your waiter today." She smiles and sits down saying, "You are a good looking waiter too." John smiles at her and puts some food on a plate for Becky.

He then dishes up lasagna and puts it on Samantha's plate with sides. Sitting next to her plate is a bowl of salad. "This looks good, John."

"Well don't wait on me, dig in."

"Not until you are ready to eat too." John is moved by her courtesy as he finally takes his kitchen apron off and fills his plate with food. Sitting down, he says, "Hope you like it."

"If you made it, I am sure I will." They begin to eat as Samantha moans, "Mmm, that is very good."

"I don't brag much, but my lasagna is awesome."

"Yes, it is. How do you like your daddy's cooking, little one." Becky shakes her head yes vigorously and eats.

Samantha asks, "Can I ask you a question?"

"Sure."

"Your coworker you talked about, Vickie, she is a beautiful woman."

"Yes, she is."

"I would think that would be a woman any guy would prefer."

"I never really thought of her that way actually. My mom liked her a lot, but even she knew that Vickie was the wrong person for me. She is the total opposite to my style of living."

"From what you have told me she is a lot like your mom."

"True, but I certainly did not want someone in my life like her. Don't get me wrong, I loved my mom. I just could not be with that every day." Samantha begins to crack a smile. "Are you saying something here?" John's face turns red with embarrassment and says, "No, no. Just saying—"

"Relax, John, just playing with you." John returns to a comfortable mode. "Sorry, I take things too serious at times."

"That is okay, John. Your wife, was she like your mom?"

John stares at his dinner plate and looks up. "No, no she was not. She was much like you."

"Not sure if that is a good thing."

"It is not like that. I'm not looking for a similar replacement if that is what you are thinking. I like you for you. You just happen to have the same qualities as her."

"Good answer." John was relieved he did not upset her. "I was worried there for a moment."

"You don't have to walk on eggshells around me. I am not planning to go anywhere. As long as you let me see you and this little angel, you can talk plainly to me. I may not like some things you say, but I am not going to leave. I have to tell you, I know it has been a short time, but I am in love with you. I am also in love with this little girl." John stares with wide eyes at Samantha. "Wow. I don't know what to say."

"I am not pushing you into anything, okay? I am just telling how I feel, and you can be honest with me, if you don't feel the same way, that is okay."

"I like you a great deal, a whole lot." Samantha holds her fork slowly, chewing and staring at John, and then she smiles. "Well that is wonderful, John." John feels like the pressure is off and continues to eat freely. After dinner, they sit on the couch watching Becky play with her cars. Samantha nestles next to John to watch his daughter. The wheels turn in a torrent of mixed emotions in John's head, but he is frightened to engage Samantha much further. Later, John watches Samantha get Becky ready for bed and tucks her in. Samantha blows a kiss to Becky as she acts like she catches it. Samantha and John walk into the living room as John says, "You are good with her."

"She is a little gem." Samantha turns and looks back at Becky's room and back around to John as he grabs her and kisses her passionately. For what seems an endless time they are locked in a slow kiss that seems to never end. Finally they slowly break apart and she says, "Oh, wow, that was great."

"Yeah, I don't know what got into me."

"Don't apologize for it. I loved it."

"You did?"

Samantha smiles and nods her head as he grabs her again and gives her another long kiss. They finally stop and gain their composure as Samantha sees he is getting embarrassed and says, "Well I need to get home, got a lot of work tomorrow."

"Yeah, me too." She walks to the door as John follows. She says, "See you tomorrow morning."

"You sure you want to carpool again?"

"You are right on the way to my work, it makes sense. Besides, I love the company."

"See you in the morning." Samantha gives him a hug and quick kiss. "Love you, John."

"Good night." She leaves as he watches her go to the car and leave. He closes the door and leans against it, blowing a sigh of relief.

⸺⸺•⸺⸺

The next day at work Vickie walks into John's office. "So how is the new squeeze?"

"Squeeze? You are so kind. She is fine by the way. Becky loves her, and she loves Becky."

"You two getting serious?"

"No, just dating. I have a daughter to worry about. She is good with her."

"What is the problem, John?"

"No problem. It is nice seeing someone socially once in a while, but you know I have to get back to real life too."

"She is not a fantasy, she is real life. As real as you want to make it."

"I know, we are just friends."

"Okay, John, whatever you say. But if you want my opinion, I think you really like her."

"What makes you say that, Ms. Psychic?" Vickie walks to the door and turns to John. "Because you haven't even told me her name yet."

"Samantha, Samantha Svetlik."

"Oh, Czech girl, eh?"

"Yes, her family is Czech. Is there a problem with that?"

"Not at all, John. *Jak se mas.*"

"That is what she said, what does that mean?"

"Ask her, she is your girlfriend."

---

A couple of days pass, and Vickie leaves the office and notices John is getting in his own car alone. "Where is your carpool jockey?"

"Oh, I told her I wanted to drive to work alone these days."

"I see." She gets in the car as John begins to explain, and she leaves. John looks down at his car with a guilty feeling and leaves. The next day, Vickie ignores him as he tries to talk to her. Finally, he corners Vickie, "What is wrong, Vickie?"

"You, that is what is wrong."

"I am fine, but you are agitated."

"You are miserable, not happy like you were before. I know you broke up with your girlfriend."

"It was not working out."

"You know what the issue is? You can't get over yourself, and you hide behind you daughter and dead wife. That woman lit you up, but I guess we will never know if she was right for you now." Vickie walks off as John mumbles to himself, "Like being around my mother all over again." The day drags on as John stares at his desk and out his window. He finally decides to leave early and drives to the cemetery where his wife is buried and visits her grave, which is close to his mom's. "Mom, I could use your strong advice these days. You apparently left me with Vickie to continue the harassment. Miss you, Mom, love you." He walks over to his wife's grave and kneels down. "I miss you so much. I feel so guilty for seeing this other woman and involving her in our child's life. I betrayed you and our daughter. I am deeply sorry for it. Please forgive me; I won't make that mistake again." John gets up and looks over his wife's tombstone into the short distance near a tree. He sees a dead bird laying on the ground and its mate standing over it. He begins to stare intently as the bird walks around the dead one in circles and looks around. Finally, it hears the chirping of another similar bird in the tree above it, and the grieving bird sees the bird in the tree. The one the tree keeps chirping as the one on the ground looks down at the dead one and then flies up to the meet the other one in the tree. They chirp and tweet and interact, finally flying off together. He watches them leave into the distance. He walks over to the dead bird on the ground and looks back at his wife's grave.

John arrives at the special-needs daycare where Samantha works and he walks in. He begins to say something to Samantha, but she cuts him off and says, "Let me get Becky." She comes back hand-in-hand with Becky and says, "There is Daddy, sweetie." Becky runs over to John as he kneels to hug her. Samantha looks on but turns around to go back to work. "Becky, that does not belong to you, you better give that back to Ms. Svetlik." Samantha turns around, and Becky runs up to her and hands her an expensive diamond ring. Becky holds the ring up to Samantha as her face looks in shock. John walks over to her and kneels next to Becky as all the employees and kids watch. Silence grips the daycare. "You are the light in my and Becky's life, and we need you. Our future depends on you and me both, let me say I love you. Can you be my wife and her mommy for the rest of our lives?" Samantha holds her hand over her mouth with tears rolling down her face. "I can and I will." John puts the ring on her finger and stands to kiss her as Becky hugs her leg. John picks up Becky, and they all hug together as a roar of clapping erupts in the daycare. "What does *jak se mas* mean?"

"It means 'how are you doing?'"

"I am doing perfectly fine now."

"So am I." They look over at Becky, and she points at Samantha. "Mommy." John starts crying. "Yes, honey, she is."

Samantha hugs Becky and cries. "I love you, my daughter."

# THE CAMPAIGN

Tom, John, and Vickie meet with Pastor John Austin and his producer Jane as well as Director Bob. They greet and sit down as Pastor Austin speaks. "So how are coming on the campaign ideas?"

"I think we have a good strategy for you and your church organization," answers Tom.

"Great, what have we got?"

"You know, I have been in the news some fighting this Lazarus Game," adds Vickie.

"Yes, that is one of the reasons that attracted us to your company. The publicity and your efforts would look good for us too."

"And we will use that. We need you to campaign against the game at your church."

"That is more a civil and political issue, and we really don't get involved in politics in our services, especially for tax reasons. As soon as you promote one side of the political spectrum, you end up splintering off some of your following," said Jane.

"I understand that, but you cannot be everything to everyone. This is an issue that everyone can get behind now; most all the companies have dropped this game. You are jumping on an issue that is all but over with and riding it to the finish line. You look like winners and become vindicated in your opinion at the end. Besides, Pastor Austin, if you have any ambitions toward politics, this would give you a track record to move into that. That is if you had any plans for that."

Pastor Austin looks at Vickie with a grin on his face. "Why, yes, there have been on occasion people tell me I should run for office."

"Well you can start making strong friends and enemies now or make them later. As for your church, it will not suffer. Sure you will lose some people, but our study shows it falls into the twenty-one to thirty-three age range, who your numbers say don't tithe. Advertisers we have lined up are not really targeting that group anyway, so it affects things little by losing them. However, the older crowd will likely embrace your new passion and stand. It will also invigorate more mature audiences that will be willing to let go of cash."

Jane looks at Pastor Austin. "What do you think, Johnny?"

"It makes sense. I think we can take the hit because it will most likely be just a dip, right?" says Pastor Austin.

"That is right," says Tom. "Our campaign focuses on your old fellowship and more mature audiences as Vickie says, but as they are cemented in your church, we start to shift the campaign to target younger people. The buzz we create should bring them all in, and when they see the way your established people tithe and act, they hopefully will follow suit."

"You know, I appreciate this tactical assessment of how to approach the campaign," says Pastor Austin. "I wish it was not so…what is the words I need?"

"Manipulative," offered Vickie.

"I am not sure it goes that far, but it does sound like it."

"I don't mince words. It is what it is. You and anybody of power lives for the ends and do anything for the means. We all rationalize it to think it is all for the better good, but make no mistake, it is manipulation. Not trying to make you feel guilty about it, just bringing the honesty so we can be clear how this works."

"I understand, I may not feel good about it, but it really is for the good of everyone." Tom brings out the contracts to proceed with the campaign as Pastor Austin grabs a pen to sign the deal. Austin looks up at Vickie. "Why do I feel like I need to sign this in blood?"

"You are." Austin laughs a bit, but then his need and ambition guide him to sign. "There we go, done."

"Fantastic," says Tom. "We will start immediately and get with Jane with the details of the campaign."

"I look forward to it," answers Jane. They celebrate with soft drinks as the Zion team leaves for the elevator. Tom and John wave them on as Vickie stares at Pastor Austin. He waves back as the elevator door closes while looking at Vickie. "That Vickie is something else."

"You are not used to a purely honest person," says Jane.

"Sadly I don't get many of those in this business. We need to be careful because she has already figured out I have political plans. A person like that can turn things against me in a hurry if she suspects a problem."

"Will there be a problem?" asks Bob.

"One can never tell. That woman is a crusader, and the problem with crusaders is they are only loyal as long as you are in line with their beliefs."

"I think we can control Vickie and anyone else that comes along," says Jane.

"I hope you are right."

Vickie and John walk back to Vickie's office. Vickie sits down at her desk as John says, "What do you think of Pastor Austin really?"

"I think he is a good man deep down. However he has strong ambition, and that can blind people to do many things they would not normally do. We serve his purpose for now, but when he runs for political office, things will change."

"You don't think he will use us there?"

"He can't. He has to demonize the evil ones that got him into power as if it was their fault. You wait and see."

"Well we are making money now though. I just think it is odd hearing this kind of stuff from a religious leader."

"I am sure he feels he is doing good in his heart. People are not always what they appear to be. So tell me, when is the big day?"

"Six months, February 21."

"Are you anxious?"

"Yes, very. Sam is a wonderful lady."

"I think she is perfect for you."

John looks to the ground. "You know, I never thanked you for pushing me to date. I would have never gone out with her if you had. I had seen her many times at the daycare and even talked with her, but it never snapped to ask her out. I almost blew it after we got together."

"All you needed was someone to tell you it was okay to be happy."

"Yeah, I feel free." Vickie smiles as John waves at her and leaves.

---

The ad campaign starts for the Lion Temple of Zion, and advertisers push a variety of products, but the last commercial during the break is Pastor John Austin asking people to join him in support of ending the Lazarus Game. After the break, he gives a few minutes to explain the game to his followers and asks them to contact their representatives and request the game be ended. Surprisingly, the stand begins to solidify his followers, and his church begins to grow in televised viewers. Letters, e-mails, and calls begin to pour into senators and representative's offices at state and federal levels. The pressure begins to percolate, causing the oversight committee on the Lazarus Game to step up and make a decision. They begin interviewing CEOs of companies and subpoenaing records of the game. After several months of hearings Vickie is called into the panel to hear the decisions of the senators. Again she finds herself with Trevor sitting in front of the senators with TV crews everywhere. "Ms. Newsome and Mr. Ortiz, thank you for rejoining us again," says Senator Adams. "There has been much discussion about this game and much support for your cause. Mr. Ortiz, did you ever think when you were in the game that you would end up here?"

Trevor looks at Vickie as she smiles back at him, "No, sir, senator, sir."

Adams has a large grin on his face. "Yes, I would suspect not." We on this panel have found this Lazarus Game, as it is called, to be violating various human labor laws as well as certain tax codes. Because of this, we have directed law enforcement under our control to investigate any further ventures of this game that are carried out from this point on. So I would advise any person or persons participating in this game to cease immediately. Further, we are sponsoring a bill that will be voted on in the next session to target and go after any further activities that uses people wrongfully as this game has. The bill is called the Vickie Act."

"Sir, may I ask one favor?" Vickie says.

"Of course, Ms. Newsome."

"Can we rename it the Trevor Act?"

Adams looks at his fellow senators as they nod. "Why, yes, we can. It will be named the Trevor Act." Vickie grabs Trevor as he looks at her with pride. "Well that is it. Do you both have anything you would like to say before we close this panel?" Trevor looks at Vickie, and she nods as he says, "Thank you, sirs, for taking this serious. It makes me proud to be part of this. Thank you."

"Thank you, senators, for ending this atrocious activity, you have done good here. Thanks to all the people that supported the ending of this game and for certain leaders of groups that came forth to support it too," adds Vickie.

"With that, I call this panel closed on the subject, and thank you for coming," says Senator Adams. Vickie and Trevor get up and hug each other as media begins to question both vigorously. "Ms. Newsome, how does it feel to bring down a huge scandal?"

"It is a great victory for those involved, not just people like Trevor here, but executives that were pressured to play in order to fit in or others prey upon them with extortion."

The reporter looks at Trevor. "You feel justice has been served, Mr. Ortiz?"

Trevor smiles. "I am glad that Vickie listened to me and had the guts to help. I mean, this could have ended her career. One thing I have learned is there is no stopping her when she gets going."

"That is good. Ms. Newsome, what is next on your list to take on?"

Vickie smiles. "I have no list. I just take things as they come." Another reporter comes up. "I understand that you are doing an ad campaign for the megachurch Lion Temple of Zion. How do you feel about the story breaking that the pastor had an affair?"

Vickie looks puzzled. "It is true we are running a campaign for them, but I have not heard anything about an affair, if you will excuse me now." Vickie and Trevor punch through the wall of reporters and people congratulating them.

Vickie and Trevor are flying back to their hometown. "Vickie, why did you take on the Lazarus Game really?" Vickie puts down a book she is reading and replies, "At first I felt like a number of people, that it was just a victimless game that had its bad points but also helped charity. After seeing how it affected you and being reaffirmed by Cindy, I saw the effects were not so good. My martial arts teacher Sato impressed upon me that there are times to take a stand no matter the cost."

"What if what you fight for is not exactly right too?"

"No side you take will ever be pure and perfect. You just need to decide what you believe in and what is worth fighting for. As long as there are human beings involved, there will never be a perfect solution. We just have to do the best we can."

"I guess so. What was that reporter talking about the pastor having an affair?"

"I am not sure, could not find anything in print that talked about it. If it is real, it must have just broken in the news."

"Will that end our business with them?"

Vickie smiles. "No, just makes it more challenging."

"We would still help his church if he is like that?"

"He is a client and pays, and we are in business to make money. We can't afford to be self-righteous about everything. That was what that reporter was trying to goad me into talking to them about. You know, after taking down the game and then representing a cheating pastor. The media likes to churn controversy over and over no matter what side or issue. That is their way of running an ad campaign."

"That sounds like advertising, not news."

"It is news, just done in a fashion to drive people's emotions. Ever notice they announce they will talk about something you want to hear about in the next segment after commercials? Those commercials are the higher-priced ones because you are glued waiting to hear about that piece of news. It is business like ours. They have to squeeze every dollar they can. I can't fault them for that. It only bothers me when they stir up masses of people that end in some kind of violence or hatred. That is a problem."

"Yeah, what is that book?"

"After talking with your dad about the Texas revolution history, I happened to see this book at the bookstore." Vickie hands the book to Trevor.

Trevor looks at the front page. "*Southern Cross.* What is it about?"

"You would like it. I will not give it away for you. But it is about a young boy in Mexico called Miguel. He loves astronomy and dreams to be an astronomer but lives in a very poor village."

"Interesting, can I borrow it when you are done?"

"I will let you have it for sure. You know, I wanted to be an astronomer when I was a kid."

"How come you did not become one, you are smart enough."

"Life had other plans for me. We don't always get to decide our destiny it seems." Vickie stares like she is looking a thousand yards away as Trevor asks, "You okay?" Vickie breaks from the trance. "Yes, I am fine, thank you." Trevor smiles and leans back to nap as Vickie continues reading her book.

# THE GUILT TRIP

A few days later the news is everywhere about Pastor Austin and the woman that is accusing him of having an affair. Her name is Christy Copeland, and she was the personal secretary to Pastor Austin. The controversy has caused the pastor's wife to leave to destinations unknown to avoid the media. Vickie travels to the Lion Temple of Zion church to meet with the pastor and his people to assess the damage. Vickie arrives at the church, which is huge and has a massive pyramid front encasing the entrance with giant dome for an auditorium. Overwhelming and massive, the structure impresses all that approach it. Vickie is met by the pastor at the entrance. "You spent a few nickels on this place."

Pastor Austin smiles. "Yes, it keeps the rain off our heads."

"Very nice glass pyramid on the front.

"Actually, it is more a ziggurat in style."

"What is the difference?"

"You see above us it has twelve levels to the top stone. The bible talks about the New Jerusalem in heaven having twelve walls, well that is what it looks like. You know twelve tribes, twelve major constellations of Mazzaroth?"

"I have heard the term *Mazzaroth* before, but okay, I will bite, what is a New Jerusalem?"

"It is a city of gold encrusted with jewels that has the tree of life in the center of it. Even the floor or streets in it are gold but transparent."

"Well that is my bible lesson for the day then." The two enter the auditorium under the dome and see a massive spread of stadium seating and multilevels leading to a stage in the very front. "This looks like a cross between an opera house and a rock concert."

"It has to be, we can put twenty thousand people in here." They walk down the stairs leading to the stage as Vickie is taken in by the opulence of the place. "I can see why they question why the money for this could have gone to feed poor people."

"If we did not put on a production as we do, there would be no place like this and therefore no audience. You have to do this to get the money to do more. Fact is we do run a number of soup kitchens around the country. A church that does not feed the hungry is no church. My dad was a pastor too when he was alive, and he always said that the church was and organism not an organization. The saddest thing he always said was that the poor and down-and-out used to go to churches for help, but somewhere along the line they became a social club. He was a real pastor."

Vickie looks at Pastor Austin. "You don't consider yourself a pastor?"

"I am a pastor, but nothing like my dad."

"What would your dad think of this place?"

Pastor Austin smiles. "If he was here, he would tell me to leave this production to other ministers and get myself on a street corner and preach where I belong. He was an extraordinary man. Eighth-grade education and no seminary but could outthink scholars. The Lord truly worked through him."

"Sounds like you miss him greatly, bet he was at least proud you became a pastor."

"Actually I was a finance auditor but after meeting my wife, she brought me to my first passion, which was to preach. She was able to get me where my dad always hoped I would be. I made the transition to preaching at small churches, and I guess my personality carried me to bigger and bigger places. Then one day I ended at this church. We took a bond and bought this place and remodeled it for our church. It just seemed like I stepped into very successful enterprise like a fast-moving train. Well till this whole affair thing broke in the media." Vickie and the pastor looked around from the stage at all the seats. "I can't imagine these seats being empty during service. That scares me. Can you help?" Vickie has felt that the pastor is a good man as she suspected all along and says, "Let's help get your train moving again." He escorts her to their offices where Jane and Bob are waiting with their CFO controller Deborah Skilling. Pastor Austin introduces Vickie to Deborah, and they sit down. "I have to ask the obvious question, was there an affair?"

"No."

"How did the media get to this indictment of you?"

"As Jane pointed out to me long ago, it was probably not a good idea to have a personal secretary that looks like a fashion model, but I did not see her as that, just a secretary. Christy was everywhere with me, and there was no issue. A few weeks ago she began to ask for bonus money. I gave her a small bonus thinking she needed the money for something but was too proud to tell me what for. I let her keep her dignity, but turns out it was not enough. She kept asking for more. So I asked her what it is for and that maybe we can solve the problem together. She said she just wanted it, otherwise, she would expose things about me. Obviously this took me aback because what could she blackmail me about?" The room is obviously tense as he describes the problem, but Vickie can detect there is something else going on but earnestly listens. "Well when I refused to pay her, she made a huge scene, and I fired her. Next thing I know media is calling me to respond to allegations of an affair with my secretary. I told them there was nothing to report and that she is just a disgruntled ex-employee. Apparently that was not good enough, so here we are."

"I don't understand how she could get this much media attention just for an accusation. If there is no proof, then the media can be held legally liable for reporting something untrue."

"It does more damage for a church to fight in court against this kind of thing; besides, we preach first amendment rights. Fighting the media over their reporting would defy what we stand for."

"I feel that is crap. So be it though. I still say the media has to have some kind of smoking gun to do this." Austin looks over to Jane as she looks back at him, and Bob just stares at the table. Deborah just stares at Vickie intently. Pastor Austin clears his throat and says, "We had a birthday party for Christy." Austin throws a copy of a picture to Vickie. "This is what she is using as proof." Vickie looks at a picture of Pastor Austin sitting in a chair with Christy sitting in his lap kissing him on the cheek passionately and him smiling.

"Looks kind of friendly for a pastor."

"Christy was excited because the pastor had given her a car as a birthday present," said Jane.

"Well that was a very nice present. A little big of a present for a secretary, don't you think? What does your wife think of this picture pastor?"

"She was the one that took the picture. Actually it was her money that bought the car for Christy. Money my wife made from her cookbooks," Pastor Austin said.

"No good deed goes unpunished it seems. Still the question remains, why such a nice present? I ask because a probing media will eat something like this up." Austin stares at the table quietly. Vickie looks around at the people at the table. Bob continues to stare at the table as Jane puts her face in her palm. "There was an affair but not with you, pastor. You are protecting someone else." Austin's face turns red, and his eyes tear up as he nods. Vickie waits for an answer as the pastor wipes his tears away. "The affair she had was with my wife." Vickie covers her mouth. "Holy crap. Sorry, poor choice of words."

"I knew about it for a little while, but my wife and I played the part of good husband and wife for the church."

"Wait, I am confused, didn't your wife make you a preacher?"

"I told you, my dad was the real preacher. I am fraud built upon a lie. My wife had a hidden passion for other women, but she was raised religious herself. Such a thing would devastate her family. She loved Christy, and I think she loved her back at first. That is why my wife gave her the car, not me. She was happy and even gave me a kiss because I hid the affair. My wife was happy during that moment. She had it all it seems. The one she really loved and a great life that we both had financially and publicly."

"You have been living under a pyramid it seems, but more a love triangle. Did your wife try to appeal to Christy in any way to avoid this?"

"She did but soon realized that she was just using my wife to extort money. There was no reason beyond money. My wife is more heartbroken than anything is why she is not around."

"This is going to tear this place apart no matter how it is told," says Jane.

Vickie stands up and paces in front of the meeting table a few times. Vickie sits down and says, "Pastor, do you and your wife have kids?"

"No, we never had kids."

"Here is what we do. You stand before your congregation next service and leak out to the media that you will be discussing this controversy with your people."

"You want me to admit to an affair and ask for forgiveness like other televised preachers have done? We have studied the numbers, and we will take a huge hit. Deborah has done an impact report."

Deborah agreed. "We will lose thirty percent of our membership initially and, depending on how the media works it and public opinion, more than fifty percent by one year. Pastor Austin will have to step down in order for this church to remain in business, and then the next person will have a challenge to rebuild it."

"So you see it is devastating," Pastor Austin said.

"Pastor, does your wife have any medical problems?"

"If you are trying to say that she is lesbian because of medical or hormonal issues, then, no."

"No I was more thinking if she had any issues with her heart where the stress could lead her to any life-threatening issue."

"No, why?"

"I think you should just go to your service and admit exactly what has happened." Austin and Jane both exclaim "what!" Bob puts his head down on the table.

"That is the absolute worst thing that we can do," said Jane.

"That is right, Jane," agrees Pastor Austin. "Deb, what are the numbers on that scenario?"

"We never explored that, so I believe we might as well close the doors if you do that," Deobrah said.

"Pastor, are you going to patch it up with your wife, what are your plans with her?" asked Vickie.

"We had no plans to leave each other beforehand, but after this, she said maybe it would be good if we divorced."

"She loves you and believes in you?"

"Despite her hidden life, she is a wonderful person, and I love her dearly. She would never hurt me personally or professionally."

"I suggest you have a long talk with her and tell her that you are going to bring it all out. I think if you explain it to her she will understand. Her family will be hurt, but they will still love her. She will be free at that point to live as she wants. Eventually for her the media will die down and forget about her."

"What do I do after preaching?"

"You will continue to preach here."

"How?"

"Sometimes tragedies are opportunities if we are smart enough to see the silver lining. Think about it, you have done nothing wrong. You have done what any good husband has done. You provided a good life for your wife, and even when you discovered her indiscretion, you protected her dignity. You are the perfect husband, she is the cheater. You and your wife became a victim of a scam that has only served to expose a secret life your wife wanted to live. However, in your world, such a life is not possible publicly. So you stand in front of everyone and tell them the truth, every bit of it. You throw yourself on the court of public opinion and let them decide your fate. I think you will find they will shun your wife and agree that you divorcing her is the best for both. It will deflate the media and discredit Christy, taking the wind totally out of their sails. You remain steadfast as the pastor, continuing forward to lead your people as the most eligible bachelor in the country. You just gained a huge female audience." They all stare at Vickie in disbelief, stunned.

"You are the living devil," said Pastor Austin.

"Don't demonize me; I am just the one that dispassionately figures things out."

"No, I did not mean that. I am just shocked."

"I understand."

"We will discuss this among ourselves of the next couple of days and let you know what we decide."

"Don't wait too long because deciding if you do this or not will affect on how much we can charge for the lead in commercials before your announcement on-air."

Pastor Austin chuckles. "Lord, help me."

"Maybe that is why I am here."

"I need to have some alone time with the Lord. Deborah, could you take Vickie back to the airport?"

"Sure, pastor," Deborah says. Vickie says her good-byes as she walks with Deborah.

"You know, your plan might just work. I hope it does because we are depending on our jobs here."

"I take it this is a good job for you."

"I have never made better than I have before, and I worked a large finance company."

"Pastor Austin must be a good boss."

"Actually he is kind of cheap but has a weakness for people."

"Obviously. Did you suspect anything about his wife before this came out?"

"I guess in the back of my mind. Christy and I used to be good friends and hung out together. She never came on to me, so this was a shock. She did not seem like she liked women, but I am not a good judge of character."

"I guess she was a good actor."

"Very good actor." Vickie is taken back to the airport but decides to stay in the hotel nearby as the details of the church scandal swirl in her head.

# PARK ANYWHERE

The next day Vickie calls Cindy to talk about this issue.
"Cindy, I have a question."

"Sure."

"You have heard about Pastor Austin and the affair accusations?"

"Yeah, it is burning up the news."

"Well I am in the town they are at and met with them. They are a client of ours and have been for a while now. What I am telling you is confidential. The reality is the secretary actually had an affair with pastor's wife."

"Holy crap."

"That is what I said when I heard it. Anyway, in your professional and personal opinion do you think that a woman that starts an affair with a rich and famous straight married woman is a real lesbian or just using her for money? Because the wife tried to patch things up, but the secretary kept wanting money only. So is she just playing lesbian?"

"She might be but mostly likely is just a user. However usually someone does not just get a job to extort or decide to do it after a while. They usually are driven because they learned it from someone or felt betrayed."

"Exactly what I needed confirmed. Thank you, Cin."

"You are welcome. You know I feel sorry for the pastor. Cheating is not an easy thing to live with, especially if your job is to watch over others. That pastor has to feel like a failure on many levels."

"He does, but we will fix that."

"Okay, got to go. See you later, girlfriend." Vickie hangs up and leaves with information in hand she had acquired from Jane. Vickie walks to the apartment of Christy, and she sees the red sports car that the pastor's wife had bought her. Vickie knocks on the apartment door of Christy and hears through the door, "No interviews."

"I am not a reporter, I represent the church." Vickie notices the peephole is being used, and then the door opens a little. Christy looks around and says, "You are that lady on the news about the congressional hearings. The one we hired for the ad campaigns."

"That is correct."

"What are you doing here?"

"I am here to talk about your money."

Christy's eyebrows rise up. "Oh, well come in." Vickie enters as Christy locks the door and says, "I have to be careful because the media has been camping out fishing for an interview."

"I am sure." They sit as Christy asks, "Can I get you something?"

"No, thank you." Vickie sees a picture of Christy and a guy holding each other on the wall. "Your boyfriend?"

"Used to be, but he left me because of my affair with the pastor."

"I am sorry to hear that. You cared for him."

"Yeah, sure, I guess. Anyway, you mentioned you were here about my money."

"Yes, I am. I have an offer for you to end this situation."

"About time they gave in, what is it?"

"If you agree to return what remainder of money you have not spent that you have extorted from the church and the car, I will agree not to have you imprisoned for extortion and conspiracy with another employee of the church."

Christy's face becomes angry. "What?"

"I know this extortion game from another, and if you don't want to go down with them, I suggest you make restitution and admit that you seduced the pastor's wife when you learned of her secret."

Christy stands up. "Who the hell do you think you are? You get out of my place right now before I beat your ass. You tell that so-called pastor he better pony up some money or this media circus will bring him down further."

Vickie stands up. "If that is the way you want it. You have meddled with a good man of God in my opinion, and even God has avenging angels."

Christy flings the door open. "You leave now." Vickie struts over to the door and turns toward Christy, overshadowing her in height and stature. Vickie smiles at Christy as she stares back at Vickie deep in her eyes. "God says vengeance is mine, but you know what? I like to do my own dirty work." Christy is speechless and shows signs of concern as Vickie smiles and leaves.

The next morning Christy looks out her door, and no media are in sight and no Vickie who she is more concerned about. She thinks to herself, *Just idle threats*. She confidently leaves her apartment and goes to the car she was given by the pastor's wife. She starts it up and starts driving down the road arrogantly, but people are moving out of her way as if she owns the road. She says, "That's right, move out of my way." She laughs, and then a police car passing her the other way turns its emergency lights on and U-turns to catch up with her. She pulls over, and the officer with his hand on his gun walks up to her car. "Is there a problem, officer?"

"Any reason for the emergency?"

"I was driving below the speed limit."

"Playing dumb? I am talking about the red-and-blue lights in the front of your car."

"What?" The officer opens her car door and asks her to follow him to the front of her car. As they arrive, she looks down and sees tiny alternating red-and-blue strobe lights hidden in front of its grill, flashing. "Officer, I have no idea how that got there. Someone is pranking me." The officer reaches in her car, looks around, and finds nothing illegal, so he pops the hood open. Another officer arrives soon and walks up to the front of Christy's car too. The second officer says, "What is up, Joe?" Officer Joe answers, "I pulled this lady over for illegal emergency lights flashing, but she claims she has no knowledge of it. I was just looking over the wiring. Looks like it was wired to where when her car is running, the lights stay on." The officer pulls the wiring and takes the lights off. He asks, "You have any idea who might have done this?"

"Yes, but I am not sure," replies Christy.

"Look, I believe you because no one would wire something like this unless it was a prank. It was meant to operate when you were in the car and started it up unknowingly. I suggest you check your car from now on and be careful of other pranks," Officer Joe says.

"Yes, officer, thank you."

"Good day, ma'am." Christy gets back in her car and starts to pull out as she says to herself, "That bitch."

Christy arrives at a truck stop diner where she meets with her boyfriend Chad. The two embrace and kiss as they sit down. "I ordered your favorite," says Chad.

"Thanks."

"What is wrong?"

"I was visited by a woman that handles my old job at the church, their marketing, Vickie. She is the one that was on the news about that company game she took down." Chad looks bewildered as Christy continues. "Never mind. She made a threat to go after me about this church affair thing and wanted me to give back money to the church and my car."

"What a major B."

"I kicked her out of my apartment, but she threatened me."

"To hurt you? Because I will kick her butt."

"No, it was not a physical threat. Besides, I don't think you could take her, she seems pretty tough-looking."

"Let me at her, I promise you there is no woman that I cannot handle."

"Well, anyway, I think she wired police lights on the front of my car last night. Because they were flashing when I turned the car on, and I did not know it. I got pulled over, and the police pulled them off and let me go."

"That was lucky."

"I know. I am glad they believed me. I was scared I was going to jail. Going to jail, you know, maybe that was what she was trying to do. Scare me with the threat of jail."

"Who, this Vickie woman?"

"Yes."

"What do we do?"

"We do nothing. You don't exist anymore, right? I need to contact my friend at the church. She can take care of it."

"Hope so, I am looking forward to us getting married and living large."

"Just a matter of time." The two get their food and eat. As they enjoy their meals, Vickie stands between Christy's car and Chad's motorcycle staring at them. After they finish their meal, they head to their vehicles. Chad makes sure Christy's car is fine and has no emergency lights on it. He checks his motorcycle as well, and they leave. Christy runs errands to the store noticing once in a while that someone is staring at her. She brushes it off and does her tasks for the day.

Christy arrives at her apartment with a storm of media people waiting for her. She steps out of her car as a reporter asks, "Miss Copeland, you have any comment about the picture of you and a man named Chad Castor at a truck stop hugging and kissing. Is this a love triangle with Pastor Austin? Does the pastor know this other man?"

"What picture?"

Another reporter asks, "Is it true that you and Chad are lovers long before you got your job at the church? How does Chad feel about you and the pastor?"

The first reporter asks, "There is a story circulating that you were extorting money from another employee of the church to keep things quiet at the church, any comment?" Christy pushes her way through the reporters into her apartment. She goes to her phone, which shows that Chad has already called her, and the phone rings. "Hello?"

"What is going on? I got back to work, and the place is storming with reporters asking about our meeting a couple of hours ago. How did they know about it?"

"It has to be that Vickie woman. She followed me and set us up. Don't say anything to anyone. I am going to call my friend at the church." She hangs up and calls her contact at the church. "Hey this Christy. We have a problem."

Deborah from Zion says, "Yes I heard the news. This is a huge problem because this discredits your lesbian thing as a threat against the pastor."

"What do we do now? That Vickie woman was here yesterday threatening me to give back money I got from the church and the car."

"What? Why didn't you tell me?"

"You told me not to call you."

"Fine, just sit tight and not worry about it. Let me deal with it on my end." Deborah leaves her office and goes to Pastor Austin's office, but he is not in there. She looks around, and one of the employees says he went toward the conference room. Deborah goes into the meeting room and says, "Excuse me, pastor..." She stops as Vickie, Jane, and Bob are there with Pastor Austin. "Come in, we were just talking about you," Pastor Austin says.

Deborah sits down. "About me, what about?"

"Vickie was telling us a theory that she believed you and Christy are in collusion on this extortion deal. She also believes you are skimming from the donations."

"That is ridiculous, I have been here long before you all were here." Austin picks up the phone and calls his IT administrator. "Karen, this is John. Can you bring the most recent phone records from our phone system? Thanks." Austin hangs the phone up as they all stare at Deborah.

"look I know you are stressed and this is a bad time for all of us, but this is no time to go on a witch hunt. Christy is the one you need to focus on." There is no response from any of them as Deborah continues, "I cannot believe this is happening. Maybe I need to call our previous pastor and have him straighten you out." Austin puts the phone on speaker phone and calls a number. The phone rings. "Hello?"

"Pastor Matthew, this is John Austin from Zion, how are you? I have you on speakerphone."

"Well hello there."

"In the room I have Jane, my executive producer, and Bob, our director of production. I also have Vickie Newsome, our marketing coordinator and Deborah Skilling, as you very well know."

"Hello, everyone." Everyone says hi, and Deborah says, "Hi, Pastor Matthew, it is good to hear from you." No response comes back as Austin begins. "Pastor, as you and I discussed in my office just thirty minutes ago with Vickie about Deborah, well, we were having a staff meeting, and

Deborah barged in. So I guess this is as good of a time as any to discuss this if you are ready."

"That is fine. Deborah, I have covered for you for many years knowing you were stealing from the coffers. But I let it go because it was not a huge impact in the scheme of the amount of money we take in, and I felt that controversy, if made public, would discourage people from giving to the church. However, I was wrong as this has led you to go further into conspiracy schemes and extortion. I am very disappointed in you, and, John, I am sorry I left this mess in your lap."

Deborah has a shocked look on her face. "Pastor, I have never stolen anything from this church."

"Not true, Deborah, as I did have a private accounting of what was missing, and I am sure an audit with law enforcement of your personal accounts will show irregularities in the money you possess. I urge you to make restitution privately and stop the extortion scheme at once, or I will be forced to testify against you in court and publicly denounce you."

"Sir, you have been bewitched by the true con artist here, Pastor Austin. He is deceiving you, and if you say someone was embezzling it was not me."

"Pastor Austin, you have my full support."

"Thank you, Pastor Matthew," Pastor Austin said. "We will be in touch." Austin hangs up and sits back. "Well, Deborah, the ball is in your court."

"You have no evidence I did anything because I did not."

"Is there any reason for Christy to talk to you after this affair issue broke in the news?"

"I don't talk to her. Have not seen her since you cut her loose."

"You two used to be close friends." At that time Karen the IT person brings a printout of the phone records. "Thanks, Karen." Karen nods and leaves, looking at Deborah. Deborah adjusts herself in the seat. "Just before you stormed in here, you got a call that lasted four minutes. The number that called here is Christy's home phone." Deborah sits staring at the table. "Well?"

"You are going to lose a lot of people donating here if they think their money is being stolen."

"I am making you this one offer, and is only good right here, right now. You quit immediately. You end, convince Christy to stop what she is doing, and go dark in talking to the media. You both quietly disappear and live your lives. In exchange, I will not prosecute anyone, and you get to keep the money you have stolen. I think that is generous. Vickie here wanted to get every dime out of you back."

"Vickie. Why did you have to come here? Everything was smooth till you came."

"What is your decision?"

"Fine." Austin puts the phone on speakerphone and calls Christy.

"Hello, Deborah?" Everyone looks at Deborah as she looks away.

"Pastor Austin here, and we have you on speakerphone with Deborah and other people in the room. Deborah has acknowledged the scheme to extort money from the church and that she has been stealing for a long time. We know everything now, and Deborah has agreed to a deal in order to keep both of you out of jail."

"Christy, can you hear me?"

"Yes, Deborah."

"The deal is we do nothing anymore to the church and quietly keep out of the media. If we do that, then the money you and I have, we can keep."

"But what about the plan?"

"It is no longer possible because the last pastor has corroborated things that would expose that plan."

"So we are done."

"I am afraid so. We just need to cut our losses and go." There is silence for a solid minute. "Christy!"

"Okay, I agree."

"Then it is done." Pastor Austin hangs up the phone and calls security to escort Deborah out and IT to lock out her access. Deborah waits for security to arrive and says, "I don't know how it ever got to this."

"I think it is easy once you do one thing it seems normal. It is like an addiction. I pray you will find yourself again."

Deborah starts crying as she leaves with security. "Thank you, Vickie, for your involvement."

"You know it is not over."

"You think others are involved?" asks Jane.

"No, pastor, you need to still make your confession before your following. You cannot trust Deborah and Christy to keep quiet. If you don't deflate this issue now, it will come back."

"We can contain it now," says Jane.

"No, she is right. That is the right thing to do. If my people are to trust me, I need to be honest with them. Also, my wife needs to be free too. Keeping silent will just continue to imprison her in a life she really does not want," says Pastor Austin.

"Sir, I hate to bring it up, but isn't 'freeing' her, as you say, going against your principles?" asks Bob.

Austin stares at the table. "Yes, very much. But we as humans are all sinners in many ways. We all have family, friends that live in ways we totally disagree with. But they are still part of us, and we have to accept they are different. We must live in this world in peace, not imprisonment. My hope is someday God will heal her of those feelings, but in the meantime she needs to be healthy enough for him to reach her. I do not want to stand in God's way."

Vickie looks at Pastor Austin with an impressed look. They leave the meeting as Pastor Austin walks Vickie out. "Service is in two days, I will make the announcement then."

"I will make the arrangements on our advertising end and public relations."

"Thank you. You know, it was all so simple when my dad was a pastor."

"I don't think it was ever simple, he just kept the solutions simple. You are a good man. A good preacher."

"Thanks, but my dad was the preacher."

"He would have been proud of you. You are a preacher." Vickie leaves as Pastor Austin watches her walk out. He looks up at his pyramid of glass and walks back into the auditorium. He sits at the backmost auditorium chair and stares at the stage to think.

# Sᴇʀᴍᴏɴs  Mᴏᴜɴᴛ

It is the day of Pastor Austin's sermon, and singing as well as other production routines move along as normal. Finally, the time for the pastor's sermon part comes up. Pastor Austin approaches the podium and looks down, seeing Vickie front in center. She smiles at him as he smiles back. The auditorium grows quiet as media is there to catch the words after all the issues have played out. "Ladies and gentlemen, you have seen and heard a lot of things in the media lately. You heard rumors of an affair between me and my secretary. Well I am here to set the record straight and throw myself at your mercy." Members of the audience gasp, thinking the rumors must be true. "The reality is that it was not me that had an affair. When it broke, I had no idea how to handle this issue. How do you handle something of this magnitude? On one hand, you have your church and flock to take care of that depends on you to be steady and guide them. On the other, you have family and responsibility as a husband to take care of your household and employees that depend on you for their jobs. You don't have the luxury of feeling pity for yourself or the ability to give up. The race is not given to the fast but the enduring." He stares down at the podium for a moment and then continues. "I am guilty of hiding the affair. But the affair was not me but my wife and the secretary."

Everyone reacts in disbelief and eventually quiets down. "I know, what a shock. My wife, first off, is a wonderful lady. She is the same lady you have seen every Sunday who comes up here and delivers her message of hope and tolerance. That is all she ever wanted to convey. She is the one who opened up soup kitchens for the poor and homeless. She is the one who convinced me to leave the world of finance and become a pastor. So she has done all these wonderful things, but does all that go away because we discover that she was not living the life she really thought she should? True, it is not our belief. It is a sin against God's commandments. But I submit to you my apology for trying to hide this fact. I did not know until an unscrupulous woman that I hired as a secretary found the weakness in my wife and exploited it for her own financial agenda. My wife truly thought she was in love with her and even bought her a car from her own book money. But soon after, this employee of ours turned on us, threatening to expose the affair, as if it was with me, if I did not pay. I in good conscience could not give her any of the church's money because that is not my money to pay extortions. That is your money. That is money for homeless people and keeping the lights on this place and reaching people as far as we can on TV. Well you all know what happened next. The media let it all out. What you don't know is what was happening behind the scenes because I and my staff did not know either. This extortionist was being directed by our own accounting controller, who has been stealing money for years, even before I have taken over this church. They planned to extort what they could, and then I would be removed as pastor so the accountant could continue to skim under new management. I spoke to the previous pastor about it. Pastor Matthews admitted he knew she was skimming some but was afraid it would keep you people from donating if you knew some of it was falling in people's pockets.

Pastor Austin takes a deep breath and starts to tear up and chokes a bit. "My wife and I are divorcing so she can find herself. I ask you to pray for her to find her way no matter what it is and no matter how much we disagree with it. I ask her family to forgive her and continue to welcome her as family." Pastor Austin stops and turns around. "Pastor Matthew, could you come out here please?" Pastor Matthew steps out and stands behind the podium as Pastor Austin stands next to him.

Pastor Matthew begins. "I apologize for letting this person take your money all those years. That falls on me and is something that bothers me greatly as towhy I retired earlier than normal. A church is such a volatile thing. It does not take much for people to leave, and their money leaves with them. Then your church and the people that work in it that depend on its income are lost. I should have been honest with you from when I was here. Pastor Austin would not have to deal with this now. Because of my fear, I put the burden on him. I only ask you forgive me and forgive him. Please do not punish him for my mistake." The pastors hug and Pastor Matthew leaves the stage as the place is quiet.

Pastor Austin speaks, "Well it is in your hands on what to do here. I cannot control your opinions. I can only say we have rectified the mistakes and will be vigilant to not allow this to happen again. If you do find it in your hearts to forgive us, I ask one favor if I may be so bold. My wife, or soon-to-be ex-wife, asks that she continue to head the project of running the soup kitchens. That was her child, and she wants to continue that ministry. I told her it was fine with me. That is if we are all still here later. If you decide that is not acceptable, I will leave too. She brought me here to be your pastor, and if she is not allowed to continue her good deed in this world, my existence here has no relevance. God bless you all, and thank you for letting me be your pastor." Music begins to start queuing up that the end of the service is coming as Pastor Austin stands steady, looking over the people. The people sit quietly with some looking at each other, then slowly they begin to leave.

Vickie walks up to the stage as Pastor Austin shakes her hand. "Thank you for coming."

"You are welcome. Good luck." Vickie leaves and as she leaves the front of the building a reporter recognizes her and asks, "Ms. Newsome, it is interesting finding you here. Were you here to know what the pastor was going to talk about?"

"I knew already because our marketing company works with them."

"Sso what do you think about the affair and extortion?"

"You know what, you will not find a better man than the one that spoke in there. You people especially in the media love to tear down anyone that trips up. You are so quick to go after celebrities, and religious leaders are prime targets. Yeah, there are bad ones out there but let's see you try to run an organization like that and keep everything squeaky clean." Vickie walks off, and the reporters try to get opinions from people coming out, but most do not want to talk.

# THE DAY OF BELLS

As the days and weeks pass Vickie's company works hard to maintain a positive image for the Zion church. Meanwhile, many other accounts come in that require their focus. It is a good distraction sometimes to work on other projects. Vickie meets with John in his office. "So the big day is coming up in a couple of months.

"Yes, it is."

"Nervous?"

"Terrified."

"So where is the wedding going to take place?"

"We are still trying to book some places, but seems like everyone is getting married when we are."

"Oh, what fun it is. Good luck." Vickie returns to her office, and she gets a call from Pastor Austin. "I just wanted to thank you for all your help. Our numbers have grown, and we are strong. Support for our church has grown better than ever. My ex-wife still runs the homeless projects, and even her family has accepted her despite the embarrassment and disappointment. I can't thank you enough. If you ever need anything, let me know."

"Actually, I have one small favor to ask."

The day ends and John walks up to meet his fiancé Samantha and Becky to leave for home. Vickie walks up. "Well, look at the soon-to-be newlyweds."

"Hi, Vickie. Newlyweds if we can find a place to get wed that is," Samantha says.

"I know a place."

"Really, where?" asks John.

Yyou would have to fly out to it, but I would pay for the whole trip there." Samantha and John laugh as John says, "Okay where?"

"How would you like to have your wedding and reception at the Lion Temple of Zion?"

"Are you serious? How?" asks Samantha.

"Well let's say the pastor owes us one, and he said he would be honored to hold your wedding there. He will even decorate the place in your style, and you can have him or anyone perform the services."

Samantha starts crying. "That place is so beautiful and huge. It would be a dream come true."

"Yeah, it would be incredible," agrees John.

"Well I will set it up for your big day and have his people contact you for the arrangements."

Samantha hugs Vickie. "That is so wonderful, thank you."

John hugs Vickie. "One from me too."

Vickie laughs. "Have a good evening." They leave waving as Vickie waves, smiling.

That evening, Vickie meets Cindy and Lisa at their home to have a nice dinner and meet. Cindy. "Girlfriend, you are back. Can you be in the media some more because we were getting bored not seeing enough of you."

"Oh, stop. How are you, Vickie?" asks Lisa.

"I am fine, and I think I am done with media for a while."

"Well food is ready so come on in as they say," says Cindy. They all sit down as Vickie says, "It has been a while since I had a vegetarian dinner."

"It is good for you," assures Lisa.

"It does look good."

"So, give us the skinny on what happened," says Cindy.

"The church thing. The pastor admitted to the whole real issue before his people and it seemed to actually pay off. His church is stronger than ever."

"You know what I am digging for."

"Yes, his wife was a closet lesbian, and the secretary figured it out and exploited it for her own financial means. The pastor and his wife are divorcing and living separate lives."

"That must be a major disruption in the whole church thing."

"It is an emotional hand grenade going off in the middle of it all. But you know what? I think they are going to be okay."

"I have a lot of sympathy for that pastor actually. It is hard on families that are straight who have to deal with the fact that gay people are in their family. We get a lot of flak from our families for it, but they are hurting and upset too. I wish there was a manual to help both sides of the fence adjust to the realities."

"Maybe you should write one. You are the professional," suggested Lisa.

"She's right," agrees Vickie.

"What did you think the first time you realized what I was in college?" ask Cindy.

"I was like, okay, as long as she keeps her meat hooks to herself, we are not going to have a problem here."

"Really?"

"Not really. It does not bother me because I am not that religious for one thing, and, two, I have seen the worst people can be, so being gay is not something that does not register on the Richter scale for me."

"So it does not bother you."

"I don't agree with your lifestyle, but what I am saying it does not bother me."

"Well technically it is not a lifestyle but mostly genetic."

"I have heard that and do not agree with it. But I do agree there are genetic propensities to favor one lifestyle or another. However we are governed by intellect, not instinct, so the final decision to be one thing or another is up to us."

"That is a good argument, but I have heard it all before."

"Well you are in a position professionally to promote your beliefs."

"Actually, I do not promote anything."

"Why not?"

"I am here to help people reach themselves, no matter what that is. It is not about recruiting people to gay or straight or religion or atheist, it is about helping them be themselves. Sometimes it means they become something that defies everything you stand for and believe. It is tempting to thwart letting that bird fly away knowing it is detrimental to what you are. However, I would not be the right person for this job if I filtered people in this world."

"That is why I love you," says Lisa.

Cindy smiles at Lisa. "love you too."

"That is good, Cin. I have heard too many people say this is right and that is right, but how do we really know? A wise man told me once that God, to a flower, is water and sunlight. To an animal, God is food, water, and sunlight. You see, it is about what you are conscious of that determines your perception. We can never know God in his totality, but he brings to us himself completely. We just get what we need and can understand."

"That is profound. However, one question though. What if God is a she?"

"Maybe gender is something only for us, who knows. Again, we only know things through the filter of our own mind."

"Who was this wise man that told you this, sounds like an eastern religion thing."

"Pastor John Austin."

"Wow that surprises me, sounds like he is progressive."

"More like open-minded."

"Well if you like him, I like him."

Lisa raises her tea and says, "To Pastor John Austin." They raise their glasses, and Vickie says, "To honest people no matter who they are." They drink and enjoy their meal. Cindy and Vickie walk to Vickie's car.

"How are you holding up?"

"You know, I was bothered by some of my more severe patients, but once in a while one gets better and it makes it all worth it."

"It sounds like you have found your peace, and that is important." Cindy and Vickie make it to her car, and Cindy hugs Vickie hard. "I love you, girlfriend, so much."

"I love you too, Cindy." They smile as Vickie gets in her car and leaves. Cindy makes her way back to the apartment to join Lisa in a quiet evening together.

⎯⎯⎯⎯●⎯⎯⎯⎯

Several months pass and the big day for John and Samantha has arrived. John arrives at the Lion Temple of Zion and sees the place fully decorated. As he walks in the auditorium, he sees the first five rows in front are set for his and Samantha's family and friends while the rest of the auditorium is full of church members that have arrived to watch the wedding. Vickie is there and greets John as maid of honor. "How are we going to feed all these people?" asks John.

"You are funny. They are not going to the reception. They are just here to support the wedding."

"Vickie, thank you for all this." They hug and John says, "Well I better get down there. John walks the long row of steps to the stage where his best man Tom, his boss, awaits, along with other members of the company. Vickie adjusts some flowers and looks around to nod her head and then heads to the stage down the row of stairs. Members of the church begin to stand and clap as Vickie walks down. She is stunned and pauses to wave as she makes her way to the stage. She walks by Tom and John as the clapping dies down, and Vickie says, "Did not expect that." John and Tom laugh as the place goes silent. Vickie smiles at Pastor Austin, who winks at her. John looks down at the front row where Samantha's mom is sitting with Becky. Becky holds a pillow with the rings on it. She smiles up at Dad, proud of her job. John waves at her with a smile, but suddenly his attention is drawn to the very back door as Samantha is standing there with the sunlight shining behind her. John is awestruck as she makes her way down with some bridemaids and her father. As they make their way to the stage, they stand in front of Pastor Austin.

"Who gives this woman away to be married?" asks Pastor Austin.

Samantha's father says, "Her mother and I do." He gives his daughter a kiss and leaves the stage to sit with his wife. The pastor begins the service as Vickie can't help but tear up. Becky is carried to the stage and walks up to her dad and Samantha holding the pillow with rings tied to it. Vickie's mind wanders as the vows are given. Pastor Austin announces, "Ladies and gentlemen, may I introduce John and Samantha Taylor. You may kiss the bride." They kiss as Vickie looks on, her mind wandering of her past love in college and imagining the pastor's words saying, "May I introduce John and Vickie Patterson." Vickie's mind focuses back on the wedding as the sounds of clapping erupts loudly and church bells ring out. The bride and groom leave as a married couple with Becky in tow to the reception area of the church. Then members of the stage follow them as family members in the rows follow after that. Members of the church leave while volunteer members stay to perform clean up and make sure the rest goes well.

At the reception Vickie walks up to Pastor Austin as both watch the festivities take place. "Thank you, that was wonderful."

"You're welcome."

"You will have no problem with your aspirations as a politician in the future."

"You know, I think I will stick to pastoring. It is what I was made for. Maybe that is something you should think about doing."

"Interesting, but politics is not my game. Your dad is proud of you, preacher."

"I know he is."

"Well I am grateful for this and your wisdom."

"It was the least I could do for our…well, um…I am not sure what to call you."

"Just a woman that lives her life and sometimes tries to pick up those that have fallen and help them get where they need."

"In Norse mythology that woman would be called a Valkyrie." The pastor smiles at Vickie and puts his hand on her shoulder, then he joins the reception. Vickie walks back to the auditorium seeing the thousands of seats. She looks at the magnitude of where people gather as something deep inside her beckons. She is not sure what she is feeling but knows there is something that lies in wait for her. Vickie smiles and returns to the reception to enjoy the fruits of her labor.

Other books and information can be found at:
www.Mazzaroth.net

If you have any comments about
this novel, please write to:

msims@mazzaroth.net

I would love to hear your thoughts.
Thank you for reading my story.

—Mike

9 780099 829838 2